When he was forced into a pregnancy, Oam knew he wouldn't be allowed to raise his child. He'd made his peace with that, but now King Eldar is gone, and Oam is a father.

Tito never wanted to be a father, but he can't say no when he's given his late cousin's egg. She wanted him to raise her child, and he will, even though it takes him away from his best friend — who happens to be the new Eiloren clan king — when Killian needs him the most.

Oam and Tito both have to learn how to be parents. It's easy enough when they're dealing with eggs, but what will happen when the eggs hatch? And when Tito and Oam fall in love?

Even with the war over, the clan's problems aren't. As if that's not enough for Tito to worry about, someone is trying to take Oam's egg from him. Tito won't allow that to happen, but can he stop it? Will Tito and Oam be able to build the family they both yearn for, or will they lose their rosy future before it happens?

Rosy Future
Copyright © 2024 Catherine Lievens
ISBN: 978-1-4874-4143-2
Cover art by Angela Waters

Published by eXtasy Books Inc

Look for us online at:
www.eXtasybooks.com

Rosy Future
Eiloren Clan 1

By

Catherine Lievens

CHAPTER ONE

Tito was about to become a father.

The thought was enough to make him want to throw up, and he might have if he'd been in the privacy of his own suite back at home. Instead, he was at the Ogorth clan, surrounded by people he didn't know. He was here for the war and was supposed to support his king through it.

There was no one better than him to support Killian. He'd been Killian's friend for most of their lives, and he'd become his personal assistant when Killian had taken his father's place on the throne. The two of them had planned the coup together, and even though it had been terrifying, it had been nothing compared to what Tito was going through right now.

He was about to become a *father*.

He swallowed and stared at the door in front of him. He'd been told the infirmary was located here and that he'd be handed the egg today. He'd been tempted to say *no thank you* and ignore the entire situation, but he owed it to his cousin not to.

He closed his eyes as he thought of her. He couldn't believe he'd never see her again, but he wasn't surprised. He and his family had been frantic since the Saganto clan had started down the path that had led to this war. Delia had become a Saganto clan member after she met her partner, Alix. She'd kept in touch with their family for a while after moving in with them, then had stopped.

They knew why now.

Tito could only imagine how frightened she'd been and

1

what her life had been like. She'd no doubt been happy when she found out she was pregnant, but instead of raising her child and settling down in her pregnancy and in her new family, she'd had to run. She'd managed to save her child, but she'd died in the process, as had her partner. The baby in the infirmary had lost their entire family, and they hadn't even hatched out of the egg.

How could Tito raise this child? How could he do the job his cousin had been supposed to do and make her proud?

When he thought about all of it, he wanted to cry. Instead, he opened his eyes, squared his shoulders, and stepped toward the door. Wasting time wouldn't help anyone, least of all him. This was something he had to do, and he might as well do it and get it out of the way.

No matter how terrified he was, there was no other option.

He pushed open the door. The space was wide, with big windows that gave it an airy feeling. There were two rows of beds, one on each side of the room. A few were separated from the rest of the room by curtains, but not the one Tito was looking for.

The egg he was here to collect didn't need a bed yet, but Lisha, the healer, had settled by one anyway. He and a human man were looking at the egg, and Tito took another moment to breathe and settle his anxiety.

There was no way to change what had happened. No matter how much he wished to, he couldn't. His cousin wouldn't come back, and neither would her partner. They were dead, and Tito was already making plans to bring their bodies back to their clan. Technically, Alix wasn't an Eiloren clan member, but that didn't matter. He and Delia had been together. They'd fled the Saganto clan and had come to warn the Ogorth clan of what their king was planning. They both deserved to be celebrated and honored. Alix would become a clan member even though he was dead.

Lisha manipulated the egg for a moment longer. Tito had no idea what he was looking for, and he probably wouldn't understand even if the healer told him.

Lisha lowered the egg. "Everything looks good."

"I know you told me about the baby, but I almost hoped you were kidding," Tito said.

Lisha set the egg down on the nearest bed and turned to Tito. He smiled at him, but it was a sad smile that echoed Tito's feelings.

Having children was almost always celebrated in their clans. The same should have gone for this egg, but instead, the baby inside had lost their parents and might hatch in the middle of a war. Tito had no idea when the egg would hatch, but he prayed it would wait a bit. He needed to be able to focus on the war and keep everything as it should be. Killian needed him, and he wanted to help.

"Unfortunately, I wasn't," Lisha said. "This baby lost both of their parents and only has you left."

Tito snorted. He'd known that, but that didn't mean he was comfortable with the idea. "Way to make all of this sound easier. You don't have to guilt me into accepting the egg. I'm taking it home."

"Good. I realize what we're asking of you isn't easy. I'm sorry for your loss."

Tito couldn't look away from the egg. He was related to the child inside of it, but he wasn't their father, or rather, he wasn't supposed to be. He'd been asked to take that role, but he was sure plenty of people would be better suited, even if he ignored his job and how much work he had because of the war. "You're sure they wanted me to take care of it? Because Delia's parents would be happy to raise their grandchild."

"It's what the egg's father told me before he passed away. I don't know if the two of you ever met, but he seemed to know and trust you."

Tito had never met Alix. He and Delia had a whirlwind romance, and no one had been able to stop her when she'd decided she wanted to move in with him. Everyone had thought they'd be happy and build a family, and maybe for a while, they had been. They'd never have a family, though. Both of them were gone, and while Tito didn't understand why they trusted him so much that they wanted him to raise their child, he would honor that.

That didn't mean he was happy about it.

"As if I needed more responsibilities," he muttered as he moved forward. "I never met Alix, but I knew of him. I was worried about Delia, of course, but I also wanted her to be happy, and that would only have happened with Alix. That's why I didn't try to stop her when she left. I wish I had now, but then I think she would've hated it. She didn't deserve to die or any of this, but she made her choices, for better or for worse." And now, Tito would have to deal with the consequences.

He didn't begrudge his cousin. She hadn't chosen to die or to abandon her child. If she'd had a choice, she'd be with the egg today, not Tito. The Saganto clan had killed her and her partner, had torn apart a family, and had orphaned a child. Tito wasn't a fighter, but that didn't mean he didn't feel the urge to find the Saganto king and strangle the old man.

Tito's hand shook as he reached for the egg. He sucked in a breath when his fingertips touched the surface. He wasn't sure why, but he hadn't expected it to be warm and smooth. He had no idea what he was doing, but the only way was forward. He'd accepted this responsibility, and he'd be the best father he could for this baby.

He looked at Lisha. "Everything's all right? Is the baby healthy?"

"I checked, and the baby's growing perfectly. They still have a few weeks, so you'll have time to get back to the

Eiloren clan and settle things."

"You make it sound easy." Tito knew it would be anything but.

"I know it won't be. It's a heavy responsibility, especially considering what's happening around us."

Tito didn't want to be reminded about the war right now. He had too much work and not enough time to do it. No matter how much he wanted to run away screaming, he had to focus on the war and what Killian would need from him.

Tito turned his attention to Christian. "I was told you found the egg and took care of it."

"I did. I was running for my life and found it in the forest. I knew I couldn't leave it there, so I brought it home and kept an eye on it."

"Thank you. If it weren't for you, this child would have been alone in the forest and would have probably died. You saved their life." Tito would never be able to repay this man enough. Hopefully, he'd find a way to once the war was over. For now, the only thing he could do was to thank Christian.

Christian was visibly emotional. "It was a pleasure. Well, it wasn't, because I wish the baby's parents hadn't died, but you know what I mean. I did what anyone would have done."

"I'm not sure that's true, so thank you again." Tito cradled the egg against his chest. It felt odd, but he'd get used to it. He'd have to. "I should go. I have more work to do before I can leave and return to the Eiloren clan. None of this was supposed to happen, and we're scrambling to find a way to work things out."

Christian stepped forward and reached for the egg but didn't touch it, as if he was afraid Tito would get angry if he did. He looked at Tito, asking for permission. Tito was glad about it and had no problem allowing Christian to stroke the egg one last time.

"The bodies are ready whenever you are," Lisha

whispered when Christian stepped away.

Tito set his expression, because if he didn't, he'd start crying, and he didn't want to do that in front of these people. They were allies, but he didn't know them well. "I'll take them back to the Eiloren clan. Alix might not have been born there, but his child will be, and this baby deserves to know their parents are close by and that they were loved."

Tito would make sure the child knew who their parents had been and that they'd been heroes.

As long as Killian and Queen Ita won the war.

Oam was about to become a father.

Technically, he supposed he already was one. He'd laid his egg a little while ago. The problem was that it had been taken from him as soon as he laid it, and he hadn't seen it again. It had taken some time after the new king took over from his father to reorganize how things were done, and even after they had, they'd had to reassign each egg to their parents. It wasn't always easy, but he was sure he'd recognize his egg as soon as he saw it.

Or at least, he hoped so.

Oam tried to ignore the hope that tightened his chest. All through his pregnancy and what had happened before, he'd known he'd have to give up his child. He'd tried to make his peace with that, but he didn't think he had. When he'd laid the egg, he'd fought with the healers who'd taken it, so much so that they'd knocked him out. When he'd woken up, his egg was gone.

But that was in the past. The Eiloren clan had a new king, and he was a much better person than his father had ever been. Oam had never met Killian face to face, and he didn't expect to, but he'd watched him from afar. They were almost the same age, and Oam had always been fascinated by the prince and his friends. That hadn't changed when Killian became king, but Oam had other things to focus on now.

Killian disliked how the Eiloren clan took care of its children, and it was one of the first things he'd changed when he'd become king. People weren't forced to have children anymore, and when they had a child, they wouldn't have to hand them over. Oam and anyone else who got pregnant from now on would be allowed to raise their child as they wanted, which was why Oam was here today.

But he couldn't seem to be able to walk into the infirmary. When he'd done so in the past, he'd been hurt. He'd been forced to have a child, and he hadn't been allowed to choose who he wanted the child with. He remembered all too well what had happened the day he'd conceived, but he tried his best not to think about it too much. It had been easier not to fight, and he hated how he felt about that, but in the end, it had made him a father. That thought would have hurt him before, but not anymore because he wouldn't have to stay away from his child.

As long as he found the courage to step into the infirmary. He wanted his egg. He hadn't wanted to become a father, and he loathed the egg's other father, but thankfully, they wouldn't have to co-parent. Rutger was dead, and Oam was happy he was.

Besides, even though Oam was conflicted about how his child had come into the world, he wasn't about to abandon his egg in the hands of Rutger's family. Every single one of them was as bad as he had been, and Oam wouldn't allow that kind of person to raise his child.

That meant he had to go inside the infirmary, get over his fears and the disgust he felt when he thought about the egg's other father, and do what was right. He was sure he could do it. The hardest step was this, and everything would go smoothly once he got it over with.

He sucked in a breath, straightened his back, and strode toward the door. He pushed it open before he could think too much about it and stepped into the infirmary. He kept his gaze firmly away from the area where he'd been held when he'd conceived, looking around for his egg instead.

Unfortunately, he didn't find the egg. What he did find were Rutger's mother and sister.

Luckily, they were empty-handed, so no one had given them Oam's egg yet, but he was sure that was why they were here. Rutger had died, and now his mother wanted his child. She was as evil as her son had been, and Oam would rather die than allow her or anyone else in that family to put their hands on his child.

He hadn't expected to have to fight today, but he didn't care. He was a father, and his only job was protecting his child and ensuring they grew up happy and good. He wouldn't allow anyone to take that from him, especially not these people.

"I really should stay," Tito insisted.

Killian had his stubborn expression on, which meant he was going to fight Tito on this. Tito could understand why, and he would have ignored his friend in normal circumstances, but these were anything but normal circumstances.

He eyed the egg, which he'd gently put down on Killian's bed. The room Killian had been given was comfortable and clean, which Tito was sure Killian appreciated. They were here to fight a war, but Killian liked his comforts, probably because he'd been born into the royal family.

Not that Tito could say anything about that. He and Killian had become friends when they were children, which meant he'd spent a lot of time with the future king. Because of that, he'd had more comforts than most of the other people in the clan.

"You need to go back," Killian said gently. "I understand why you're wary of doing that, but what good are you going to be here? You need to focus on the egg, and maybe even more importantly, you need to take your family home. They deserve it."

Tito closed his eyes. "My place is here with you."

Tito felt a hand on his shoulder and leaned against Killian. Killian wrapped his arms around him and hugged him tight. Tito knew that some people suspected there was more between them than friendship, but there never had been. They loved each other, but it was a brotherly bond, nothing more. Tito couldn't imagine anything worse than being in love with Killian and becoming his consort. The thought was enough to give him hives.

"You know I never intended to bring you along," Killian said. "I don't want to put you in danger and risk losing you. If anything were to happen to me, my mother would have to take my place on the throne, and she'll need you."

Tito opened his eyes, turned, and glared at Killian. "Nothing's going to happen to you."

"I don't *want* anything to happen to me, but we're at war. We have to face the fact that something might and plan for what will happen if it does. There are at least a few of my siblings who would think nothing of killing my mother to take her place on the throne. I don't want that to happen. I don't want my mother to be hurt, and I don't want the clan to go down that path again. Not all of my siblings are assholes, but most are, and they wouldn't be good leaders."

Tito knew Killian better than he knew himself sometimes. Killian felt he wasn't ready to be king and that he never might be. He was always afraid to do something wrong and put the clan in danger, but that hadn't stopped him from supporting the Ogorth clan through this mess. Partly, Killian had felt he had to after what his father had done, but he also wanted to be on the right side.

He was.

Killian kissed Tito's forehead, then stepped away. He turned to the egg, and if Tito hadn't seen it with his own eyes, he wouldn't have believed how tender Killian's expression was. Killian had never talked about having a family, but he and Tito had been focused on other things until now. They still were, but watching Killian with the egg made Tito wonder if maybe Killian was finally thinking about the future. He'd refused until now because it was what his father had wanted, but his father was gone.

Killian turned back to Tito. "Go home. Take this child and their parents back. I'll be fine. I have Birch and Marlin, and you know they won't allow anything to happen to me. I'll call you multiple times a day if it makes you feel better. I just think you need to be with your family right now."

He was right, even though Tito didn't want to accept it. As much as he loved his job and Killian, the egg was his priority now. That baby would be his entire life for the next few years, as it should be. Tito needed to keep the baby safe, and the only way to do that was to take them home. "You *will* call me multiple times a day," he warned.

Killian nodded. "I promise."

"And you'll stay out of trouble as much as possible."

"I'll do what I can."

That wasn't good enough, but it was the only thing Killian could promise. Tito understood that even though he didn't like it. "You have to win this war and come home in one piece."

Killian's smile was gentle. "I'll do everything I can to make that happen."

Tito took the egg and held it close to his chest. It was an awkward feeling, but there was no way out of it. "I'll go home. I don't like it, but you're right. This child *is* my priority."

"I'll warn everyone so you don't have to deal with their questions. I wouldn't worry too much, though. The queen has everything in hand, and I'm sure she'll lead us to victory."

She'd better, because Tito wouldn't hesitate to yell at her if she didn't. He wasn't afraid of kings and queens.

After leaving Killian, he rushed back to his room. He'd only just arrived, and his things were still packed. It took him a few minutes to get them together, and the entire time, he couldn't stop thinking about Killian and what would happen now.

They couldn't allow the Saganto clan to win, and they wouldn't.

Tito had a lot of things to do. He kept an eye on the egg the entire time, but it was hard to focus. Maybe it was good that he was headed back home because he wasn't sure he'd be much help if he stayed. His attention would be on protecting the egg and the baby inside of it, which was what he was supposed to do as a new father but not as the king's assistant.

As soon as he was done gathering his things, Tito ordered his bags to be taken upstairs to the landing pad. Then he went to look for Birch and Marlin. They were Killian's personal bodyguards and friends, and while Tito had no doubt they'd do their job perfectly, he still needed to touch base with them.

Once that was done, there wasn't much else for him to do. He and Killian would call each other every day, and Tito could do his job as well from home as he could from here. The only difference was that he'd be far from the war, which was the best thing he could do for himself and the egg.

Tito knew that if he found Killian again to tell him he was leaving, there was a chance he'd change his mind. It wasn't only that he was leaving his king behind to face the Saganto clan. It was that he was leaving his best friend here, and he didn't know how to deal with that. He couldn't imagine a life without Killian and hoped he never would have to live it.

They *had* to win this war. Tito wouldn't have it any other way.

Oam knew the moment Filicia noticed him. Her expression hardened, and like always when she looked at him, she appeared disgusted. Oam had no doubt she believed he was below her and that he wasn't a good enough father for her son's child. He wouldn't have chosen Rutger to have a baby with if he'd had a choice.

He hadn't had a choice. She knew it, but she didn't care. She thought anyone would be happy to have children with her precious son, and she'd never cared that he was a violent asshole who couldn't take no for an answer. Oam had never understood what Rutger saw in him, and he didn't care. He never wanted to think about the dragon again.

Unfortunately, it looked like he'd have to. There was only one reason for Filicia and her daughter to be here, and it was the egg. They wanted it.

But it wasn't theirs to take.

Oam squared his shoulders and got ready for a fight. Filicia wouldn't let this go without one, and she had many more friends than Oam had ever had. Her family also had money and influence, which could mean the egg would be handed over to her. Oam wasn't sure what he'd do if that happened, but he told himself not to think about it. He wouldn't unless it happened.

"What are you doing here?" Filicia snapped.

Her tail swished behind her, betraying her anger. She quickly wrapped it around her waist, but knowing that he had that effect on her made Oam feel stronger. "I'm here to pick up my egg. What about you? Are you or Juvia injured?"

Filicia raised her chin. "We're here for *Rutger's* egg."

"Uh. I thought only the parents could pick up the egg."

"I'm sure the healers will make an exception. They'll know who I am and who Rutger was."

"I'm sure they will, but I'm the egg's father. Why should they hand my child to you?"

"Because you're not capable of being a father to my grand-child."

Oam gritted his teeth. He didn't care what she thought of him. She didn't matter. "I'm not sure why you think that, but I assure you you're wrong."

A door opened, causing all three of them to turn. The dragon who came in wore the healers' pendant, and Oam steeled himself. He didn't care what Filicia or this dragon thought. He was here to get his child back, and he wouldn't let anyone take them from him.

The healer looked up from the tablet they were carrying and blinked. "Yes?"

Oam quickly stepped forward before Filicia could say anything. "I was contacted by someone here who told me to come pick up my egg."

The healer smiled. "Of course. Why don't you tell me your name so I can go and grab it for you?"

Filicia cleared her throat. "That won't be necessary. My name is Filicia. I'm sure you know of my son, Rutger. He's the other father of this egg, and he would have wanted his child to be raised by his family, not by *him*. We'll be taking it."

The healer frowned. "I don't understand."

"There's nothing to understand, healer."

"Alcen. The orders King Killian gave are clear. The eggs are to be handed over to their parents if they're alive and agree to take them." He looked at Oam. "Do you want your egg?"

"Yes. I'm here to pick it up."

Alcen nodded. "Then I'll give it to you as soon as we check the documents together." He turned to Filicia. "Is there anything else?"

Filicia looked like she wanted to hit Alcen.

Oam was ready to bet she'd only restrained herself because it would make things more complicated for her, but he wished she would. She'd show who she really was to everyone who didn't know yet. Oam didn't think it would change much, but at least people would know.

Juvia put a hand on her mother's arm and leaned closer to whisper something. Oam wished he could hear what it was in case it involved him and their future plans. He knew them well enough to be sure they weren't finished trying to get his baby, but he had no idea how they'd go about it, and that made him nervous.

Filicia raised her chin and glared at Oam and Alcen. "This isn't over. You're not fit to raise my grandchild, Oam, and I'll make sure the people in charge of this clan are made aware of that. Once they know, you'll have to hand over my grandchild, so enjoy the short time you'll have with them. Hopefully, you won't be able to do too much damage, since the egg hasn't hatched yet."

Filicia turned around and strode away from Oam. Juvia was right behind her. She hadn't looked at Oam once, which was fine with Oam. He didn't want anything to do with anyone in that family.

"Sorry about that," he said as he turned back to Alcen.

The healer smiled. "It was clearly not your fault. Besides, I'm used to dealing with unpleasant people." He hesitated. "Will you be all right? Should I ask someone to keep an eye on you or them?"

"I don't think they'll try to take my egg by force." No, that wasn't the way they worked. They'd go to the influential people in the clan and cry on their shoulders about Oam being a terrible father and taking the egg from them. He wasn't sure he'd win this fight, but he had to try. He'd been forced to get pregnant and become a father. Filicia hadn't cared about how he felt, and she still didn't, but she hadn't counted on him deciding to keep her from raising his child.

"Let's go to my office," Alcen said as he put a hand on Oam's arm and gently turned him. "We'll go over the paperwork."

Luckily, it didn't take long. The old king had refused to let parents raise their children, but that didn't mean he hadn't kept precise records about which egg and child belonged to whom. Alcen only needed a few moments to confirm that Oam was who he was and identify his egg. When he went to look for it, Oam started bouncing his knee. He wanted this, but he was nervous.

"Here you go," Alcen said as he came back in.

Oam sucked in a breath when he saw the egg in the healer's arms. He'd only seen it once before it had been taken from him, and just like the first time, he was relieved to see there were no signs of Rutger in its color. The egg was pastel blue, just like Oam.

His hands shook when he reached for it. He didn't know what to expect, but considering how the egg had come to be, he'd never anticipated how *right* it felt as soon as his fingertips touched its surface.

Alcen let go of the egg, and Oam cradled it against his chest. He looked down at it in wonder. He'd often wondered how he'd feel about his child and if he'd be able to forgive how he'd gotten pregnant and who the child's second father was. Now, he knew none of that mattered. This was his child, and that was the only thing that did.

"Thank you," he murmured.

"It's my pleasure. I was never okay with the way King Eldar did things, especially the breeding program. I'm glad it's over and that I can reunite children with their parents. You'll have to come back regularly so I can keep an eye on the baby and their growth, but that goes for every parent. I'd also like you to call me when the egg starts cracking so I can keep an eye on it as it hatches. There's nothing that hints to there being any kind of problem, though, so I don't want you to worry. You and your child have been reunited, and *that's* what you should focus on. Be happy and raise them with love."

Oam could do that. He had no idea how to be a father, but he didn't think anyone did. It was a job to be learned through trial and error, and he was ready for it.

Or at least, he hoped he was.

CHAPTER TWO

Tito was torn about being back home. On the one hand, he was glad to be here instead of surrounded by a bunch of strangers and to be away from the war because it meant he'd survive. It also meant that the egg strapped to his chest would be out of danger, which was why he'd left the Ogorth clan palace.

But he'd also left his best friend, and he didn't know how to deal with that. For most of his life, he'd spent every day with Killian. He'd supported Killian as he dealt with his father, and together they'd taken over the clan after things had gone too far. Tito was supposed to be by Killian's side now, too, but instead, he was home. He didn't have a choice, but that didn't mean he didn't wish he did. He wished he were with his best friend right now.

He couldn't be, and he had to accept that. He didn't want to come to resent the egg because of that. The child had nothing to do with this mess and wasn't at fault. The baby had already lost enough. They didn't need a father who resented them for something they couldn't help.

The Eiloren clan palace was smaller than the Ogorth clan's home, but Tito liked it that way. The Ogorth clan was massive next to the Eiloren clan, with so many people that it made Tito's head hurt when he thought about the logistics of leading such a big clan.

He lowered over the landing pad and wrapped his wings around himself as soon as he touched the ground. He was home.

There were visible signs of the recent escape of the Ogorth clan members who'd been imprisoned by Killian's father. Part of the palace was still being rebuilt, so it was a mess, but this place would always be Tito's home.

As soon as he shifted back, several dragons rushed toward him. He'd left his assistant with Killian, but that didn't mean he was without help here. They weren't who he dreaded seeing, though. He wasn't at all surprised to see his family gathered at the edge of the landing pad. He'd told them he was coming home, and they'd been relieved, but the pain was stronger.

He gave a few orders to have his bags taken to his suite and his office readied, then steeled himself for the onslaught of words and feelings coming his way.

The first person who reached him was his mother. She threw her arms around him, and for a moment, he allowed himself to revel in this small comfort. When he and Killian had left the palace, he'd wondered if he'd ever come back. He hadn't expected it to happen so soon, and he didn't like it, but it wasn't his mother's fault. She was happy to have him back, because it meant her son wouldn't get hurt. He was unhappy because he'd never forgive himself if his king and best friend died and he hadn't been there to help.

"Thank the sky, you're back," his mother said as she leaned away to look at him.

Then she glanced down, and her gaze caught on the egg. Her expression turned sad, and Tito prayed she wasn't about to start crying. He never knew what to do when she did.

"I am," he said gruffly. "The flight was long, so maybe we could head to my suite?"

"Of course. Sorry for jumping you like this, but I had a hard time believing you were really coming back. You were so set on helping Killian that it was hard to believe you'd leave him behind."

"It wasn't an easy decision. I had to face the fact that I'm a father now, and my place is wherever the egg is safe."

Tito's mother frowned. "You know, no one expects you to take this on. If you don't feel ready for it, I could take care of this baby. I tried talking to your aunt and uncle, but they don't feel up to raising a child after what happened to Delia. That doesn't mean *you* have to take the baby."

Tito bristled. His mother meant well, but she made him feel like he'd be incapable of taking care of a child. "Delia chose me for a reason. I might not know what that reason is, but I won't betray the trust she put in me. She wanted me to become a parent to her child, and that's what I'll do."

Even though Tito didn't know what to do with the egg, the thought of anyone taking it away from him made him panic. He clung to it, even when his mother gently tried to pry it out of the carrier on his chest. She wasn't trying to steal it, but it felt like it, and Tito wasn't willing to hand it over.

"This will be the only way for you to become a father, after all," a voice drawled.

Tito briefly closed his eyes and prayed for patience. The problem was that he'd need an infinite amount of it when it came to Killian's siblings.

It was a small miracle that Killian had grown up the way he had. He was a nice man, a good friend, and a great king. His mother had raised him the right way, and it was impossible to see traces of his father in him.

The same couldn't be said for most of Killian's half-siblings. He had too many for Tito to remember all of them, but he kept an eye on every single one. He'd expected at least a few to start trouble after the coup, so he wasn't surprised to turn and find himself in front of Pearl. Killian's sister was a few years younger than he was, and she had none of his goodness.

"Don't you have anything better to do than to bother me?"

Tito asked as he turned away. He had no intention of giving Pearl what she wanted. He wasn't sure what that was, but he could imagine all too well.

"Don't turn away from me! I might not be the queen, but I'm still my father's daughter."

Tito arched a brow at her. "Do I have to remind you that your father isn't the king anymore? And before you say anything about being Killian's sister, you know better than I do how little he cares about you."

"Tito," Tito's mother cautioned.

Tito didn't need her to intervene. No matter how snobbish and cruel Pearl was, there was nothing she could do to him. She might be King Eldar's daughter, but he was the present king's best friend and personal assistant. Killian wouldn't hesitate to choose him over Pearl any day, and she knew that. Tito also had more power than her, and it would be better for her to remember that.

"You can't say that to me," Pearl snapped.

"I can say whatever I want to you, and I'll continue doing so if you bother me. Personally, I hope you'll take this as a warning and never talk to me again, but if you do, you should remember I'm not afraid of you. I won't hesitate to talk back, and I couldn't care less who your father was."

Tito had better things to do. He turned toward the dragons who had flown back with him. Two of them hadn't shifted to their human form. They'd carried the bodies of Tito's cousin and her partner, and Tito tried to avoid looking at them as he explained what he needed.

"My mother will tell you where to take them," he said. He turned to her. "Take care of them."

Her expression told Tito she was about to cry, meaning he had to leave. He felt like he might, too, and he couldn't afford for anyone to see him that vulnerable.

He especially couldn't afford for Pearl to see him like that.

Luckily, his mother seemed to understand, because she nodded. "I'll let you know," she whispered.

Tito was glad the egg was securely strapped to his chest. His arms were free to hug his mother, and while it was awkward with the egg between them, they managed. "Thank you. I don't think I'm up for doing this," he murmured.

"You already have enough to deal with. I'll take care of them."

She kissed Tito's forehead like she always had when he was a child. He sucked in a breath, and after making sure he wouldn't break down in front of everyone, he straightened his back, squared his shoulders, and strode toward the palace entrance.

He never looked back. He didn't have a reason to and didn't want to start crying like a baby at the sign of Delia's and Alix's wrapped bodies.

He walked into the palace, eager to get to his suite. He already had work piling up, even though he'd just arrived at the palace, but it could wait long enough for him to clean up from the long flight and settle the egg.

He turned a corner, already making a mental list of everything he had to do when he almost collided with someone. The other dragon danced out of the way just in time, and Tito looked up to tell them to be more careful. The words died on his lips when he found himself looking at a dragon carrying an egg, just like he was. It wasn't a sight often seen at the palace, but hopefully, Killian's decisions about how the clan would deal with pregnancies and children now that his father was gone would change that.

Oam recognized the dragon in front of him right away. Everyone in the clan knew who Tito was. He was always by Killian's side and ran the palace with an iron fist. Oam had no idea what to think of him, but he didn't know him, and considering who Tito was, it would probably be for the best if Oam didn't bring too much attention to himself.

He quickly stepped back and bowed, keeping his gaze on his feet. "I apologize," he murmured.

Oam had noticed something when he'd almost crashed against Tito. Tito was carrying an egg.

That made two of them. Oam was terrified that Rutger's family would try something, so he carried his egg everywhere. The egg hadn't left his side since the healer had handed it over, and Oam didn't think that would change anytime soon. It would be a long time before he felt comfortable leaving his child—if it ever happened. He knew Rutger's mother would come for him with everything she had, and he hoped it wouldn't be enough, but he didn't have a lot of faith in that. She had much more power and influence than he did.

That didn't mean he was giving up.

"You have nothing to apologize for," Tito said.

"I'm sorry," Oam repeated because he didn't know what else to say.

Tito huffed a laugh. "I really hope you're not, but I understand. Is that your egg?"

Oam blinked and allowed himself to look up. He'd seen Tito from afar around the palace and always thought the dragon was handsome. That hadn't changed, even though he could see that Tito was tired. He'd flown to the Ogorth clan palace with their king, then had come back. That was a lot of distance over just a few days, so Oam wasn't surprised by the dark shadows under Tito's dark magenta eyes.

He nodded quickly. "It's my egg, yes."

"Are you one of the people who are getting their children back?"

"Yes. I don't know how to thank you and the king for this. I never expected to get my child back, and it's a dream come true." Oam clutched the egg to his chest, silently berating himself for being such an idiot. Tito didn't care how he felt. Why should he? Tito didn't need him to blather on about his egg. He needed Oam to leave him alone.

But Tito was smiling. "Killian will be happy when I tell him about this. He's trying hard to fix his father's mistakes."

"He's doing a good job as far as I'm concerned. I wouldn't have my child back if it weren't for him."

Tito stared at Oam for a moment before nodding. "Good. Now, if you'll excuse me."

Oam quickly stepped aside to let Tito pass. He watched him walk away, wondering what had just happened. His brain was having trouble wrapping his mind around this and what it meant.

Nothing. That was what it meant. It wasn't like he and Tito had suddenly become best friends, and they'd probably never talk again. That was fine with Oam. He found Killian and Tito intimidating even at a distance, and talking to Tito had made him feel like he wanted to throw up most of the time. The two of them weren't supposed to talk to each other. It had been a fluke, but it was over, and part of Oam was relieved.

But another part of him wondered if maybe he should have brought up Rutger's mother and how she was going to try to take his egg from him.

CHAPTER THREE

Tito kept glancing at the pouch around his neck where he kept his phone. He knew Killian wouldn't call during the funeral, but he was worried. Every minute that passed, he wondered what his friend was up to and what was happening with the Saganto clan.

Not being there was hell. Tito had expected to be annoyed because he couldn't do his job as well from here, but he hadn't expected the deep fear that something would happen to Killian while he wasn't with him. He remembered Killian's plans all too well. If he died during the war, Tito would have to protect Killian's mother when she took his place on the throne. She would be surrounded by sharks who wanted to take her down and eat her up, and Tito wasn't sure he could protect her from that.

Luckily, it wasn't something he had to worry about now. He'd heard from Killian a few hours ago, and everything was perfectly fine. Killian had told Tito to focus on his family and the funeral, which was what Tito was supposed to do. His cousin and her partner deserved his full attention, but it was hard.

He stroked the egg with one hand. It was smooth and warm, and it fit perfectly into the carrier. He should probably leave the egg in his suite, but he didn't trust people enough. This was his clan, and he'd grown up here, which meant he knew how bad some of the clan dragons could be. Killian's family especially wouldn't hesitate to try to take away Tito's child if it meant they could influence him or force him into doing things, and he wasn't willing to risk it. That meant the egg was with him at all times.

He didn't mind, but he'd have to find an alternative after the egg hatched. It was easy for him now because the egg was still and silent, but when it hatched, he'd have to take care of a wriggling baby dragon.

The thought terrified him.

He brought his attention back to the funeral. His aunt and uncle stood to one side, both of them crying. It hurt to see them. Tito had brought their daughter back, but he didn't feel it was enough. She should be alive. She should be the one holding the egg.

His gaze drifted to the two bodies laid out side-by-side on the ground. They were surrounded by fresh flowers, and even though they were dead, they looked peaceful. Someone had linked their hands together, and Tito took it as a sign of how much they'd cared about each other. It made it easier to ignore the wounds on both their bodies.

But Tito knew what had happened to them. He knew how they'd died, and he wished he could get revenge for them. Instead, he was here, taking care of their child. It was his job. Killian would take care of the rest, and, along with the Ogorth clan, they'd make sure the Saganto clan paid for what they'd done to Delia and Alix.

Tito barely listened to the priest's words. The dragon wasn't here for him, anyway. They were giving comfort to Tito's family, which was how it should be.

"It is now time for you to shift and send your daughter and Alix back home," the priest said as they turned to Delia's parents. "I know it's hard, but think about how happy she will be there. Think that eventually, you'll be reunited with both of them."

Tito screwed his eyes shut. He didn't believe in the afterlife, so he didn't think he'd ever see his cousin again. That wouldn't stop him from doing everything he could to be a good father to her child. It was the last thing she'd asked of him, and he wouldn't betray her.

When he opened his eyes again, his aunt and uncle had shifted. They stood shoulder to shoulder, facing the bodies on the ground. Everyone else, including Tito, took a step back.

Tito swallowed as his aunt sobbed once. In her dragon form, the sound was loud, and hearing it made Tito's eyes burn. He didn't want to cry in front of all these people, even though they were his family. He hated anyone to see him vulnerable. The only person he was comfortable crying in front of was Killian, and Tito would keep things that way. He'd need to be seen as strong to support his best friend through whatever happened next.

Tito's uncle raised his head and roared. The sound reverberated in Tito's bones, but even though he wanted to close his eyes again, he forced himself to watch as his uncle and aunt blew fire on Delia and Alix's bodies. The bodies were engulfed in flames that quickly consumed the flowers covering them, and hopefully, as the priest had said, that would take them home.

The funeral was over so Tito could move on to the next part of his day. It wouldn't be easy, but focusing on everything else would help him not obsess over losing Delia. The best thing he could do for her was keep her child safe, which meant winning the war. Tito would have time to grieve once it was over.

For now, he needed to push his pain to the back of his mind and focus on helping Killian.

Tito's aunt and uncle shifted back to their human form. Tito's uncle gathered Tito's aunt into his arms and held her close as she sobbed. They stayed by the fire, staring at the empty husk that had once been their daughter. Tito had to look away because seeing so much pain made him want to scream.

They deserved privacy, and everyone started drifting away. Tito's phone vibrated in its pouch, and he quickly took it out. He was once again glad he had a carrier for the egg because it meant his hands were free.

"I didn't expect you to call," he told Killian when he answered.

"Shit. Are you still at the funeral?"

"It just ended."

"I'm sorry for your loss, Tito."

"I know. Can we not talk about it?"

"You'll have to, eventually. You can't keep all that pain inside."

"I'll talk to you as much as you want once you're home. What's happening?"

Tito noticed his mother moving closer. He twisted to the side when she reached for the egg, then turned to glare at her. What did she think she was doing?

"You need to get back to work, and I thought it would be best if I took care of the egg," she murmured.

"Killian, wait a second," Tito said before lowering his phone. "The egg isn't bothering me, and I can work around it."

"I'm sure you can, but you shouldn't have to. I'll take care of it."

Tito trusted his mother. He understood that she wanted the best for him and that she was trying to give him what she thought he needed. That didn't mean he liked any of it. It felt like she was trying to take his child from him, and while he probably shouldn't feel so strongly about the egg since he'd only just gotten it, he did.

He was a father, and he wouldn't let anyone shoulder his responsibilities.

"I'll be fine," he told his mother.

"Are you sure? Because it wouldn't be a bother."

"I am. Thank you for offering, though."

Tito wasn't sure he had everything under control, but this was his life now, and he had to learn how to deal with everything at once. He needed to do so while the egg was still an egg ,because it was easier, and hopefully when the egg hatched, he'd have a better handle on things. Hopefully when the baby came out, the war would be over.

Tito couldn't allow himself to think about what would happen if the war dragged on. He didn't think it would, but the alternative might be worse. He could lose his best friend and a lot of the people he cared about.

That wasn't something he wanted to consider. For now, he'd focus on making Killian's life easier from a distance and praying that everything would be all right. It had to be.

Oam was panicking. There was no reason for him to, but he couldn't help it.

He stared at the egg next to him in his nest. What was he supposed to do with it? How was he supposed to raise a child on his own? How this child was born might not matter, but if it had been a wanted pregnancy, Oam would have had time to plan and decide how to raise the child.

He'd always known the egg would be taken from him. Because of that, he hadn't allowed himself to make plans or hope. It had hurt too much. Now, though, he was a father, and he had no idea what to do with any of this.

Should he take special care of the egg? Was there something he should do with it apart from being careful it didn't get hurt?

Oam's heart raced, and he found it hard to breathe. He told himself to stop being an idiot, but he needed answers, and he didn't have a partner to turn to. There were only a few people he could think of that he trusted with his egg, and as he scrambled out of his nest, he knew who he'd go to.

He could go to his family, but they were still cautious when it came to the egg. It was as if they didn't know what to do with it or how to behave. Oam understood why, since they knew how the egg had come into being. They were aware of the fact that Oam had been forced to get pregnant. Oam didn't understand why they cared about that so much since he didn't, but it was their hang-up to deal with, not his.

He had hang-ups enough of his own.

He grabbed his egg and strapped it to his chest. It had taken him a few days to remember these carriers existed and another day to find one available. For some reason, every dragon who should have had them had sold them all—or maybe Rutger's mother was making Oam's life harder.

He didn't care. In the end, he'd gotten his carrier, and he settled the egg inside it as carefully as possible. The thing was padded so the egg wouldn't break, but he still felt like it might if he breathed too hard in the egg's direction.

Oam was careful when he left his room. He expected Rutger's mother to try to snatch the egg from him, but no one confronted him or attacked him on his way to the infirmary. Once there, he was relieved to see that the place was empty. Many clan members had followed Killian to the Ogorth clan, so the palace felt too big.

Alcen was reading on his tablet, but he looked up when he heard Oam. He blinked as if he couldn't remember who Oam was, then smiled. "I didn't expect to see you so soon. Has something happened?" He put down his tablet and moved toward Oam.

Oam shook his head. "Nothing happened except that I started freaking out about not knowing how to raise a child."

Alcen's smile was gentle. "Well, it makes sense that you don't know how to do that. This is your first child, and you're young."

Oam swallowed. Was this a bad idea? Was Alcen about to try to take his child from him with the excuse that he was too young to know how to raise them? Filicia had attempted to convince him of that the other day, and maybe Alcen believed her. He'd been ordered to give the egg back to their parents, and he had, but that didn't mean he had to like it or that he couldn't try to take the egg away if he believed that Oam was incapable of taking care of it.

"Why don't you sit down and tell me what's on your mind?" Alcen suggested as he gestured at one of the beds.

Oam sat. So far, Alcen hadn't tried to take the egg. He'd been sweet and nice, but Oam still expected something bad to happen.

"Why don't you tell me what you're afraid of?" Alcen suggested.

The words poured from Oma's lips. "I don't know how to be a father. What am I supposed to do once the egg hatches? I'm supposed to care for a child, but most days, I don't feel I can even take care of myself. What if I do something wrong?"

"I have no doubt that you will. Every parent does things wrong. Being a parent is a learning curve, and you can't start learning until you become one. Have you thought about reaching out to other parents? Maybe people who have an egg at the moment? It might be good for you to talk to them and confront your fears with theirs."

Oam's mind flashed back to Tito. *He* had an egg.

But it was ridiculous to think that Oam could talk to him. Tito was the king's assistant and friend. He and Oam were so far apart it wasn't even funny.

"You think it might help?" he asked. He might not be able to talk to Tito, but there had to be other parents waiting for their egg to hatch. Maybe Oam could talk to them.

"A lot of them will be in your situation." Alcen hesitated.

"They probably went through the same thing you did regarding the pregnancy. I'm not saying your experiences will be the same, but they'll understand you better than many people could."

Oam knew what Alcen wasn't saying. Most of the people who had an egg of the same age as Oam's had gone through the same horrible experiences as Oam. Even if some of them had wanted to become parents, they probably hadn't been allowed to choose who they wanted to have their child with, and they'd have had their egg taken from them as soon as they laid it. Oam wasn't sure he wanted to discuss those experiences, but maybe he didn't have to. He just wanted to focus on his egg and how to raise his child as best as he could.

It wasn't going to be easy. He didn't know what he was doing, and part of him feared that Rutger's mother was right and that he'd be incapable of raising his child. Growing up with her would be worse, but who was to say that Oam would do a good job? He didn't want to ruin his child, but the voice in the back of his head kept telling him that he would.

Alcen reached forward and quickly squeezed Oam's hand. "I know you're scared, and that's completely normal. Every new parent is scared, if not terrified, that they'll do something wrong, and most of them do. No one is perfect, Oam, but your child doesn't need perfection. Your baby will need you to love them, care for them, and protect them. As long as you can give them that, you'll be a good father. Besides, you're not in this alone, are you? How does your family feel about you having a child?"

Alcen's question made Oam's smile. He'd felt alone in this since he'd gotten pregnant, but he wasn't. His family had supported him through all of it, and they would continue doing so. It looked like Alcen would, too, and that made Oam feel better.

"This is your child, Oam," Alcen continued. "There's no

one better than you to know what they need and how you should raise them. Don't let anyone make you believe otherwise. This egg belongs with *you*."

That was the one thing Oam was convinced of. His child belonged with him, and he wouldn't allow anyone to take them away, not even Rutger's mother. He didn't care how much influence she had or who she was friends with. This was Oam's future and his happiness, and even more importantly, it was his *child's* future and happiness. Oam was ready to do anything to ensure his child had a good life.

That meant keeping him away from Filicia.

CHAPTER FOUR

"Send them whatever they need," Tito ordered.

Samsa nodded. "I'll review all the messages and ensure everything is packed."

Tito checked the time. He had an appointment at the infirmary, and he couldn't miss it. He still had a lot of work to do, but he was looking forward to having the egg checked. He trusted the Ogorth clan and their healer, but he was anxious, and he knew he'd feel better once the egg had been checked again.

"The guards are leaving tomorrow morning, so make sure everything is ready by then," he said as he got to his feet.

Samsa would make sure his orders were followed and that everyone who'd followed Killian to the Ogorth clan palace had what they needed. It would be easier for Tito to deal with all of this if he were there, too, but he wasn't. He was far away from the war and Killian. He was doing what he could, but it didn't feel like enough.

He was overwhelmed. Usually, he and Killian worked together, but Killian had to focus on the war, which meant that Tito was in charge of the clan. Some clan members didn't like that. Tito wasn't the king, so he shouldn't be the one they had to talk to if they needed something. Frankly, he didn't care. He had Killian's trust and talked to him multiple times a day. What more did these people want?

Tito would much rather focus on the egg and on getting Killian and the others back from the war safely. Since he couldn't do that, he was focused on making sure they had everything they needed. From what Killian had said, it shouldn't be long until the war ended, and Tito couldn't wait for everyone to return.

"I have to go," he told his assistant. "Take care of this, and if anyone asks about me, tell them to make an appointment."

She grimaced. "Some of them won't like it."

"I don't care what people like or don't like."

That made Samsa snicker. Tito wished he could smile like that, but he was too worried. Still, as he hooked the carrier around his chest and slid the egg inside, he couldn't help but smile.

Fewer children would be born now that Killian had changed the clan laws. They were always small miracles, and there were plenty of children in the clan at the moment, but Tito expected their number to go down. There were other recent parents, though, like the man Tito had met in the hallway. Tito hadn't seen him again, but he was curious.

The Eiloren clan was much smaller than the Ogorth clan. That didn't mean it was small, though. There were lots of members Tito had never talked to, and that dragon was one of them. Tito wanted to look for him, even though it was ridiculous. Why should he look for this dragon? To talk about their eggs?

Tito frowned as he walked. Why not? He needed someone to talk to about the challenges of becoming a father. Killian would usually be the person Tito went to, but he couldn't understand in this case. He didn't have children yet, and while he'd need them if he wanted an heir, he wasn't ready to talk about it yet, let alone have any. Besides, he was busy with the war, and Tito would never distract him with his complaints. No, the best would be to find other new parents, but the thought of talking to people he didn't know made Tito shudder in horror.

Except this one dragon.

There had been something in their eyes that made Tito want to find them. He didn't know the dragon's name. He didn't even know if they were male or female. He knew nothing about them except that they had an egg and had recently been reunited with it. He could probably ask the healers, but that would feel like an intrusion.

By the time Tito reached the infirmary, he'd worked himself up. He'd decided not to ask the healer for details about the dragon, but he still wanted to find them. It felt like a breach of privacy, but being who he was, he had access to the lists of dragons who'd become parents recently. He'd had to compile the list after he and Killian had taken over the clan, but he hadn't looked at it since. It was the healers' job to contact the parents, and while Tito had made sure the logistics to reunite parents with their children were in place, that was where his job had ended.

Tito's phone rang before he could open the infirmary door. He didn't hesitate to take it out from its pouch and was relieved to see it was Killian. He didn't think the healer would mind if he was late for the appointment. He was talking to the king, after all.

"Please tell me you haven't done anything stupid," Tito said when he answered.

Killian laughed. "Me? Have you ever known me to do anything stupid?"

"Yes, which is why I'm scared." Tito knew Killian loved the fact that he treated him like he was nothing special. He always had, but then, they'd met when they were children, and back then, Killian *had* been nothing special. Now he was their king, but Tito wasn't about to change the way he treated his best friend.

"Well, something did happen, but I didn't start it, and in the end, we won, which is all that matters, right?"

Tito sucked in a breath. That didn't sound good. "Tell me."

No one else would have dared to order the king around, but Killian was used to Tito doing so.

"We won, Tito."

Killian's voice was soft, and Tito wondered if he'd heard that right. "What?"

"I didn't share it with you, but we knew when and where the Saganto clan would attack, thanks to Delia and Alix. We were ready for them, and we won. They managed to get to the palace, and Ita will have to rebuild parts of it, but the war is over."

Tito didn't know what to say. He was relieved the war was over, but he was also pissed. "You mean you knew what was going to happen, but you didn't tell me?"

"I wanted to, but you're so far away that I didn't think it would help. You would only have been anxious, and you didn't need that. You have enough on your plate. Besides, everything went well."

Tito closed his eyes and leaned against the wall. As soon as Killian was home, he was going to strangle him. "You mean you could have been killed, and I wouldn't have known something was happening?"

"Well, when you say it like that, I can see why it would've been a problem, but I wasn't killed. I'm coming home."

"You weren't killed by the Saganto clan, but you will be by *me*. What the fuck were you thinking, Killian? I'm supposed to know every step you take and everything you do. You can't hide that you're about to attack the Saganto clan from me, dammit."

"Technically, I didn't attack them. They attacked us."

"Don't give me that bullshit. I know they were planning to attack, even though I didn't know what day it would happen. You attacked them before they could attack the Ogorth clan."

"Why are you so angry? The war is over, and that's all that matters."

He wasn't wrong. The war was over, and Killian had survived. This was the best possible outcome to this mess.

But Tito couldn't stop thinking about the fact that his best friend could have been killed, and he wouldn't have known it was happening. "You're so fucking stupid and impulsive," he snapped. "We're in this together, remember? That's what you promised when I agreed to help you take over the clan. We're supposed to work together, but you hid this from me."

"I'm sorry I did, but I'd do it again if I had to. I can't be your priority anymore, Tito. You have that baby to focus on, as it should be."

"That doesn't mean I don't want to know that my best friend is going to war, asshole. What do you think would've happened if you'd been hurt? How do you think I would have reacted?"

"But it would have been over by then."

"Exactly! I would have hated it. Don't ever do that to me again, Killian. If you do, I'm leaving." It wasn't an empty threat. Hopefully, the Eiloren clan would never have to fight again, but just in case, Tito wanted Killian to know what would happen if he behaved like an idiot.

Tito loved Killian, but he wouldn't allow his friend to do something like this again. His heart wouldn't survive it.

Alcen and Oam looked at each other. Alcen looked amused, but Oam was worried. He bit his lower lip. "Do you think someone should go out there and make sure he's all right?"

Alcen shook his head. "I think it's pretty obvious he is. He wouldn't be yelling at the king if he weren't."

Oam had no idea what was happening when he first heard a raised voice outside the infirmary, but Tito had been loud enough that he and Alcen knew what was happening now. He was yelling at the king in a way no one else would dare, and it gave Oam palpitations. He didn't understand how anyone could talk to the king like that, even though he knew the history between King Killian and his best friend.

The king wouldn't do anything to Tito. Oam wasn't worried about that. It sounded like Tito might need support, though, and while it was ridiculous to think that Oam do that for him, he wanted to try.

"I just wish we could hear the other side of the conversation," Alcen said as he looked at the door. "It sounds like things went well."

Oam hoped the war was over, and it sounded like it might be. He might not have been personally involved, but the Saganto clan had been a danger to their clan. They would have taken over the clan if they had won the war, which wouldn't have been good for anyone.

Alcen leaned back over the egg. "Let me finish this so you can head home."

Oam hovered close as Alcen manipulated the egg. He trusted the healer but still didn't want to be too far away from his child. The fear that someone might jump out from behind a bed and steal his egg was strong, and he couldn't help but wonder if it would ever fade.

So far, Rutger's mother hadn't done anything, but that didn't mean she'd given up. Oam was sure she hadn't and that she was plotting, and in some ways that was more frightening than having to face her. She knew many people and had a lot more influence than Oam could ever have.

He looked at the door behind which Tito was still talking to Killian. He didn't know Tito well, or at all, really. They'd bumped into each other in the hallway, and that was it. The way Tito had behaved had made it evident that he was interested in Oam's egg, though. Maybe Oam could appeal to him and explain what Rutger's mother was doing. As long as he could show that he would be a good father to his child, Tito had to be on his side.

"Everything looks good," Alcen confirmed, pulling Oam back to the moment. "They'll be ready to hatch soon."

Oam blinked. "Really?"

"I don't want you to start panicking because there's no reason to. Yes, the egg is almost ready to hatch. You've known this would happen, and it's okay. They're ready for it, and you're ready to become a father to a baby dragon."

"I'm not sure about that."

"I am."

Oam snorted. "You don't know me."

"You're right. I don't know you beyond the few times we've spoken, but those times were enough to show me you'll be a good father. You worry about it, which is more than a lot of people can say. I can see that you want the best for your child and that you'll do everything you can to give it to them. To me, that's enough."

It was good to have someone outside of his family who believed in Oam. Oam's family had to believe in him, but Alcen didn't. The fact that he did told Oam that maybe he *was* ready to be a father.

And if he wasn't, he'd have to make himself ready. His kid wouldn't wait for him to feel like he was.

"Queen Ita has everything under control, but I still want to stay a bit longer," Killian explained. "There's a lot of cleanup to do and many meetings to attend. I promise I'll be home as soon as possible, though."

"It's fine," Tito assured him. "I was freaking out about you being with the Ogorth clan because of the war. You can stay there as long as you feel you need to. I have everything under control here."

"I know. That's why I'm not worried about the clan and

what's happening over there."

It touched Tito to know that Killian had so much faith in him, but it didn't surprise him. After all, no one knew Killian better, just like no one knew Tito better than Killian, not even his family.

"I'll keep you up to date about everything going on. I have a meeting to go to, though."

"And you decided to call me right before it started? Why?"

Tito could hear the smile in Killian's voice when he answered. "Because that way, I'd have an excuse to hang up if you yelled too much."

"I swear, when I see you, I'm going to strangle you."

Killian laughed. It had been a long time since Tito had heard him so lighthearted, and it felt good. Everyone had been overworked and worried since before the Saganto clan had decided to take over the dragon world. Tito and Killian had to deal with taking over the throne and Killian becoming the Eiloren king, which hadn't been easy, either. It looked like everything was going to be all right, though, and for the first time in a while, Tito felt he could relax.

He looked down at his chest. Well, he could relax for now, but the egg would hatch eventually, and the time for relaxing would be over.

"I'll record the meeting and send you the recording so you can hear what's been said," Killian told Tito. "And you don't actually want to kill me. Think about how much work you'd have if you did."

"You're not funny," Tito grumbled.

"I happen to think I'm very funny. I really have to go now, though. I'll call you once the meeting's over."

Tito had half a mind to threaten to yell at him some more then, but he probably wouldn't. He could finally stop being afraid of what would happen to his best friend. Killian was fine, and soon he'd be home. Once he was, they could start settling down and focus on the Eiloren clan.

Tito wasn't looking forward to that. He'd managed to keep enough things from Killian so that Killian could focus on the war, but he couldn't do so anymore. Killian had to be aware of the Eiloren clan's many problems to start fixing them. He was going to be pissed when he found out that Tito had hidden so many things from him, but Tito had done what needed to be done. It had been vital that the king focus on the Saganto clan because if he hadn't, it could have meant the end of the Eiloren clan. Killian wouldn't have needed to worry about their clan's problems if it didn't exist anymore.

But the bigger threat was over, and it was time to deal with everything else.

Tito returned his phone to its pouch and finally focused on the egg. He was late for his appointment and hoped the healer wouldn't hold it against him. He quickly pushed open the door, expecting Alcen to glare at him, but he found him talking to another dragon.

His gaze went to the egg the other dragon held. He would recognize it anywhere. It was pastel blue, just like its parent.

Tito had found the dragon from the hallway.

He smiled. He didn't know anything about the dragon, but he would change that.

"There you are," the healer said when he looked up and noticed Tito. "Oam and I heard your conversation. I take it everything's all right with the war?"

Tito wasn't surprised they'd heard. He wasn't angry. They hadn't been listening in. He'd been loud enough for half the palace to hear what he was saying, and that was his fault.

Well, it was Killian's fault for being an idiot, but still.

Tito moved closer. "The war is over," he confirmed. "I don't have many details yet, but Killian will be coming home soon."

Alcen nodded. "That's good. I was worried about our

king."

"Killian is fine," Tito promised. "Hello, Oam," he said, moving his attention to the other dragon.

Oam's skin was pale, so the flush on his cheeks was obvious. "Hello. Alcen is done checking my egg, so I'll give you the room."

"You don't have to leave in such a rush. In fact, why don't you stay? I don't know about you, but I don't have many people to talk to about suddenly becoming a father."

Oam looked up. His eyes were the same color as his egg. They were beautiful, like a lake Tito wanted to swim in.

He almost snorted out loud. He was being ridiculous. Oam was gorgeous, but there was no reason for Tito to wax poetic about him.

Oam's smile was gentle, and it made Tito want to make him smile even more. He wanted to fix everything wrong in Oam's life, because he could tell a lot was. It was obvious in the way Oam clung to the egg he was holding and how he held himself.

"I'll wait for you," Oam promised.

Tito almost told him to wait in the room, but Oam quickly walked away after saying goodbye to Alcen. He was visibly uncomfortable, and Tito didn't want him to be.

Alcen cleared his throat. "You're not being discreet."

Tito snorted. "I wasn't trying to be." He took the egg out of the carrier. "What can you tell me about him?"

"Not a lot. There's a lot of pain in him, which is understandable considering what happened to him."

"He told me he'd just gotten his egg back."

Alcen nodded. "You know what that means."

Unfortunately, Tito did. Taking an egg from their parents left an indelible wound. The fact that there might be more pain depending on how the egg had come into the world didn't help. Tito wanted to know, but he doubted Alcen would tell him even if he asked. Besides, if anyone was going to tell him Oam's history, it had to be Oam himself.

Hopefully, Oam would still be there when Tito was done with Alcen. If he wasn't, Tito would have to find a way to track him down.

He watched as Alcen manipulated the egg, gently knocking on it and checking the surface to make sure it was unharmed. Then he raised it up so he could look through it.

Tito had been doing so himself regularly. It always made his heart race when he saw the tiny dragon inside the egg. He couldn't wait to meet the baby, but he was also terrified by that thought. He had no idea how he was supposed to raise a child, but he would have to find out soon.

"Everything is going fine," Alcen confirmed. "Just like Oam, you don't have long to wait."

"Both eggs will hatch at the same time?"

"Around the same time, yes. Everything looks good, so you don't have to worry."

Tito took the egg back and gently placed it in the carrier. "Thank you. When do we have to come back?"

"How about next week? It doesn't matter which day. I can work with your schedule."

"I'll let you know as soon as I hear more from Killian. I don't know what's going to happen in the next few days, but it'll be a mess." Tito would have to organize the trip back for the king and everyone who had gone with him to protect the Ogorth clan and fight the Saganto clan.

"Not a problem." Alcen hesitated. "I'm sorry for your loss, Tito. I know you probably don't care about what I think, but what you're doing is commendable. It would have been easier to leave the egg with Delia's family and avoid all these complications, but you didn't. You're a good man."

Tito was used to being close to the center of attention, but this was awkward. He didn't know if he was a good man like

Alcen seemed convinced of. He just knew that his cousin had wanted him to raise her child and that the least he could do was honor her last wish.

No matter how hard it would be.

Oam had no idea what to expect. Part of him wanted to run home and hide, but Tito had asked him to wait, so he would. The other dragon probably just wanted to talk about babies or something like that. Oam didn't understand why he'd want to talk to him of all people, but it looked like their eggs were close in age, so maybe that was the reason.

The infirmary door opened, causing Oam to jerk away from the wall where he'd been leaning. Alcen and Tito were talking, so hopefully Tito hadn't noticed how awkward Oam was. Alcen did, but he smiled at Oam, so that was all right.

"I'll see you next week," Tito told Alcen before turning to Oam. "How about we walk together for a bit?"

Oam had no idea what was happening, but he nodded. He was glad the egg was secure in the carrier because he suspected that he would have fumbled it otherwise. He didn't know how to behave with Tito. Tito was a fellow Eiloren clan member, but he was also the king's assistant and best friend. It was intimidating. It was especially intimidating because Oam had no idea what Tito wanted from him.

"I'm happy to hear the war is over," he said to start a conversation.

Tito huffed. "So am I. I can only imagine what Killian got himself into while I wasn't there to keep an eye on him."

"The two of you are close."

Tito's smile was gentle. "We are. We've been close our entire lives, and leaving him behind was hell. I was so anxious that something would happen to him and I wouldn't be there to help."

"But everything went well even without you."

"It did. I'm still going to yell at him when he comes home, but it's a relief to know he's all right." He looked down at the egg on Oam's chest. "I don't know much about you, but I know enough to be aware that you didn't expect to get your egg back. How are you feeling about being a father so suddenly?"

Oam knew a bit about Tito's situation. Everyone in the clan knew about Tito's cousin and what had happened to her. Oam was sorry the baby had lost both their parents, but Tito would raise it to the best of his ability. He was a force to be reckoned with, so Oam was pretty sure the child would be fine.

He wasn't so sure about his own child. It wasn't just that he doubted his ability to be a father, but also the trouble he had with Rutger's mother. She could do a lot of harm, and he had no idea if he could fight it. Being friendly with Tito would help if it came down to that, but Oam despised feeling like he was manipulating him.

"It was both a shock and a relief, and it was fine until Alcen gave me the egg. That's when the panic started," Oam admitted.

"I understand that all too well. I never expected to become a father. I didn't know my cousin wanted me to raise her child if something happened to her, and I didn't expect her to die. I was worried when the Saganto clan started working against the Ogorth clan, but I didn't think it would come down to a war."

"I'm sorry for your loss," Oam murmured. He thought it was great that Tito had stepped up and accepted the egg. Considering his job, it couldn't have been easy, yet he hadn't backed down.

"Thank you. The thought of raising this child is terrifying, but at the same time, how could I give them up? This is what

Delia and Alix wanted, and I wish to honor that. Besides, I'm luckier than most. If I ever need anything, I'll have plenty of help." Tito looked at Oam. "What about you? Will you be raising this child on your own?"

"My family will help me." Oam hesitated. He wasn't sure that bringing up Rutger right now would be a good idea. He didn't know if Tito knew how he'd gotten pregnant and what had happened after that, and he didn't want to talk about it. They barely knew each other, and this wasn't something Oam talked about with the people he loved, let alone someone he'd just met.

Tito nodded. "That's good. My family will help, too, but I feel I need to do it myself. I'm not sure that makes sense, but I feel little does when it comes to this situation."

"Having your family help you doesn't mean you won't be doing it yourself," Oam pointed out. His family was willing to help, and they would, but they were weird about the baby. Oam suspected it was because of the way he'd gotten pregnant, but he didn't know how to help them get over it—or how to get over it himself.

Tito grinned. "The egg is my responsibility, and I can deal with it, especially because it means no one else will have a say in how I raise the child. It would be good to be friends with someone who understands what I'm going through. Why don't you come to my office for lunch tomorrow? We can eat and talk for a bit."

Oam didn't know what to say. He hadn't expected Tito to ask him to lunch, and he didn't know what it meant or if it meant something more than eating together. "I'm sure you have better people to eat lunch with."

"Other people, yes, but I wouldn't say they're better, and they haven't just become surprise fathers. I'm not going to force you, but I'd be happy if you were willing to spend some time with me."

Oam wanted to say yes, and it wasn't only because he felt he needed to become friendly with Tito in case Rutger's mother attempted to take his child from him. He liked Tito, and he wanted to get to know him better. He had no idea where that would take him, but he wouldn't know until he tried, would he? Besides, it was only lunch.

Oam nodded. "I'll come."

"Good. Will you give me your number? Just in case something comes up and I have to cancel."

Oam would have given Tito his number anyway, but it made sense that was why Tito wanted it. He nodded, and when Tito took out his phone, he rattled out his number. He didn't expect Tito to call him, but it felt odd to know that the dragon could call him at any time.

Oam needed to remember who Tito was. He was the king's best friend and his personal assistant. He and Oam didn't live in the same world, even though their paths had crossed. Oam doubted that would last long. Tito was anxious about becoming a father and needed to talk about it, but Oam was sure that once the egg hatched and things settled down, Tito would realize he had nothing to freak out about. Besides, once the king returned, Tito could talk to him, since they were friends.

But in the meantime, Oam would take this opportunity to spend time with him. Even if the only thing that happened was that Tito helped him with Rutger's mother, it would be enough. Oam didn't need them to become best friends. He just needed a little help, and there was no one better to give it to him than Tito, considering his position.

Rutger's mother wouldn't know what hit her.

CHAPTER FIVE

When Oam left his room, he felt he might be making a mistake. He didn't understand why Tito had asked to see him for lunch. They were so different that spending time together didn't make sense, and Oam didn't know how to explain it.

It had to be because of the egg. From what little Tito had said yesterday, he didn't know how to deal with being a father. Oam could understand that all too well, and Tito probably realized that. He needed to talk to someone, and who better than a dragon in the same situation as he was? Oam had no idea what he was doing with the egg, and neither did Tito.

But Tito didn't have to deal with someone trying to take his child away. Even if he did, the king would be on his side. No one would be taking Tito's egg away, but Oam couldn't be sure the same went for him, which was why he was careful as he walked down hallways and turned corners. He expected Filicia to jump out from behind a curtain and snatch the egg. He wouldn't put anything past her.

Oam doubted she'd try to take the egg herself, though. She was too dignified for that, or at least, that was what she liked to think. She wasn't too dignified to try to take Oam's child by any means necessary, though. So far, she'd been quiet, but that wouldn't last, and Oam hated not knowing when she would strike.

He swallowed as he turned another corner. He'd never been in this area of the palace. He's never had a reason to. It was where the royal family lived, and Tito had moved here as

48

soon as Killian had become king. The offices were here, too, but Oam had never needed to visit them, either. He hadn't wanted the attention of the old king, because if he'd had it, it wouldn't have ended well for him, and he hadn't had any reason to meet Killian face to face yet. He might have to if Rutger's mother continued in her quest to steal his egg.

This area of the palace was more luxurious. There were more decorations on the wall, and it felt airier. Oam had to resist the urge to peek out the window and take a few minutes to enjoy the view. He didn't want to make Tito wait. It would be better to keep him happy in case Oam needed him to help with Filicia.

The throne room was in this area, too, and Oam passed by its massive double doors. Being here made him nervous, so he gave it a wide berth and continued on to the offices. He wasn't sure where Tito's office was, but he could guess it was close to the king's.

He continued walking until he found an open door. He peeked in, not surprised to see that before he could see Tito, he'd have to deal with his assistant. The dragon looked up from their desk, noticed Oam, and waved him forward.

"Hi. I'm Samsa, Tito's personal assistant. You must be Oam."

Oam blinked. "I am."

"Tito has been talking about you."

Oam didn't know what to make of that. "He has?"

"Well, he didn't say much beyond the fact that you were coming for lunch. He had to so I could order for both of you."

That made sense. What didn't was that Oam felt happy that Tito had told his assistant. Telling her she needed to order lunch for two didn't mean that Tito and Oam were close. "Thank you."

Samsa's smile widened. "You're very welcome. You can go in, but he still has a bit of work to do, so don't be offended if he doesn't look at you right away. He's been distracted lately."

Tito didn't look like the kind of person who was easily distracted, but Oam could guess why he was. Having a surprise child would do that to someone.

He was careful as he stepped closer to the door Samsa had pointed at. It was closed, so Oam quickly knocked before turning back to her. She nodded, so he opened the door, even though it felt like he shouldn't.

The room he walked into was large. The wide windows allowed a lot of sunlight to stream in, and some of it landed on the egg that was nestled in a bundle of blankets and pillows on one of the couches. Seeing it so well protected made Oam smile as he turned his attention to the person who had put it there.

Tito was behind a massive desk that held a computer and a bunch of documents, along with several cups of coffee on it, a sure sign that Tito had been hard at work for at least a few hours. He raised one finger so that Oam knew he'd noticed him, but he didn't look up from the sheet of paper in front of him. Oam couldn't see what it was from where he stood, but he didn't want to know. It was none of his business. Tito wouldn't appreciate it if he tried making it his.

Since Tito was busy, Oam continued looking around. The egg was on one of the couches in the small sitting area by one of the windows. The coffee table there was clean and empty, unlike the desk.

The wall opposite the desk was covered in shelves, all heavy with books. Oam stepped closer to check what Tito liked to read. He wasn't surprised to see it was all nonfiction. There were history books, including one about their clan's history. There were books on politics that Oam was pretty sure would bore him to sleep and what looked like philosophy books. It wasn't Oam's cup of tea, but it made sense for a king's assistant to read that kind of thing.

"Sorry I waved you off," Tito said.

Oam turned to face him. "You're working. I'm not offended, and your work is more important."

Tito got up from his chair and stretched. Oam quickly looked away. He didn't want to, but he wanted to be caught staring at Tito even less.

Tito was a handsome dragon. He wasn't very tall, but neither was Oam. The contrast of Tito's pale human skin and his dark magenta hair, eyes, and dragon skin made Oam want to touch him. He already knew what the dragon skin patches felt like since he had similar ones on his body, but it felt like it would be different if he were touching Tito.

A lot of things would be.

Tito strode toward the door and poked his head out. "Have you ordered lunch?"

Oam couldn't see Samsa, but he could hear her. "The food will be here in a few minutes."

"I don't know what I'd do without you."

"Probably starve to death and lose your head somewhere."

Tito laughed and stepped back into the office. Oam didn't know what to do with himself, but he felt like an idiot just standing there, clutching his egg to his chest. It was in its carrier, so Oam could let go, but it felt like a shield he needed so he could face Tito and whatever would come next.

"Why don't you sit down?" Tito asked in a soft voice. "There's no reason for you to stay on your feet since we're about to eat. I hope you don't mind eating on the couch. I usually do when I don't eat with Killian."

Oam quickly nodded and obeyed. He still didn't understand why Tito wanted to have lunch with him. Why, when the king was his best friend?

It had to be because of the eggs. Tito and Oam were in similar situations, and their babies would be about the same age.

Maybe Tito wanted them to be close so his child could have friends. Oam did, but he imagined that Filicia wouldn't make it easy. She'd probably try to send anyone Oam became close to running, and Tito was one of the few people who would stand up to her. She might be influential, but he was the king's best friend. He was strong and sure of himself and knew his place in the clan.

But something told Oam there was so much more to the king's assistant than what Tito allowed the clan to see.

Tito couldn't remember the last time he'd felt so awkward. Probably when he'd been a teenager and hadn't known how to behave around people. He and Killian had already been best friends back then, and Tito had only felt comfortable with him.

He wasn't a teenager anymore, and this was ridiculous. Tito wanted Oam to be comfortable with him and for them to become friends, and he should be better at making it happen. Instead, he felt like he was about to jump out of his skin.

Oam sat down, the egg still in its carrier.

Tito wanted him to put it down and relax, but something told him that it would be better if he let it go for now. Oam would put down his egg when he was comfortable doing so. It had been taken from him right after he'd laid it, so it was understandable that he wasn't ready for that. It probably felt like it would be taken again if he let go.

Tito sat in front of Oam and tried to think of something to talk about. He supposed he could default to the war effort and tell Oam the latest news he'd gotten from Killian, but that didn't sound like a great topic of conversation for lunch, even though it wasn't a date.

Tito wondered what he could do to make it a date. Would Oam be against that? He was skittish, but Tito was starting to realize it had nothing to do with him, or rather, not with him as a person. He suspected that Oam was intimidated by the fact that Tito was the king's personal assistant. A lot of people were. But Oam hadn't hesitated to come to lunch, so maybe there was hope for whatever was growing between them.

"You look tired," Oam said before his eyes widened, and he pressed his lips together. "I'm sorry. I shouldn't have said that."

"You should say it if it's true, and it is. I *am* tired." Tito was exhausted. It wasn't just the war effort, especially since that was over now. Killian wasn't home yet, but Tito didn't have a reason to be worried about him anymore. The king was with the Ogorth clan and had Marlin and Birch, which meant he was safe. Tito would trust them with his egg's life, let alone his best friend's.

"Is it the egg?"

Oam's tone was so gentle that it caused Tito to break down. He'd been trying to be strong for everyone, to appear as if he knew what he was doing, but he was lost and loathed feeling that way. "In part. I never expected to become a father, and I certainly didn't expect it to happen like this. The only reason I have a child is that my cousin and her partner died, and I hate that. I would rather have her alive and well, and every time I look at the egg, I'm reminded that the baby will grow up without their parents. It's not fair."

To Tito's surprise, Oam leaned forward and put a hand on his knee. It didn't feel creepy but comforting.

"It really isn't," Oam agreed.

Now that Tito had started talking, he couldn't stop. He raked a hand through his hair, wondering if he should at least try. He didn't want to spook Oam or burden him with his problems, and it would be best if no one knew the kind of a mess he was in.

The words poured out before Tito could make a decision.

"I don't know what I'm doing with this egg, and I don't know if I can do this. How can I be a parent when I don't know how? My mother raised me, so maybe I should have accepted her offer to raise this child, too. She knows what she's doing."

"It's not what your cousin wanted."

Tito was relieved that at least Oam understood him. "*Exactly*. That's what I told my mother. Delia's parents don't feel up to raising another child, especially after everything, and I get that, but I don't understand how Delia could think I would be a good father. I mean, we hadn't seen each other after she left the clan."

Tito squeezed his eyes shut. Delia had always been his favorite cousin, and he missed her fiercely. Before, he'd told himself they'd see each other again soon, but now he knew they wouldn't. She was gone.

He rubbed his face and looked at Oam. "I'm sorry about that."

Oam frowned and leaned back. Tito wanted to tell him to put his hand back on his knee, but he didn't dare. Oam looked displeased, and Tito didn't know why. He wanted to fix it anyway.

"Why are you apologizing?" Oam asked.

"Because you came here to have lunch and talk about babies, and instead, I burdened you with my feelings, and you have to deal with me freaking out. No one should have to do that."

"I don't mind," Oam assured Tito. "Besides, I understand why you're freaking out. Our situations might not be the same, and I can't know how you feel about losing your cousin, but I never expected to be allowed to keep my egg, just like I didn't expect it to be returned to me. The last few months have been hell for me, and while it wasn't the same hell as yours, it doesn't mean you haven't been through a lot."

"I have no clue what I'm doing. I don't know how to be a

father." Tito hated that.

He always knew what to do. He was the one who planned everything and made sure to have backup plans, too, but he didn't think he could plan being a father.

"I don't know how to be a father either," Oam said. "Maybe we can learn together. You have to remember that you're not dealing with this alone, Tito. You have your family, and there's Killian. I'll help you, too. As long as you don't mind that I'm as much in the dark as you are, anyway."

Tito leaned forward and grabbed one of Oam's hands. Oam's eyes widened. Tito squeezed Oam's hand. He wanted to do a little more, maybe kiss Oam and find out how he tasted, but it was too soon. Oam was wary and afraid, and while Tito didn't think he was afraid of *him*, there was something there, and Tito wanted to find out what it was.

"You'd do that for me?" he asked.

Oam quickly nodded. "We can rely on each other. We both need it, and we're both hesitant about allowing our families to help, so maybe this is how we should do it. We can be two fathers who support each other."

"I'd love that." In fact, Tito felt it was the best outcome. He and Oam could learn how to be fathers together. The two of them might make one competent parent.

Even if they didn't, they'd learn how to be better.

Together.

CHAPTER SIX

Tito couldn't say everything was going well. He supposed he *could* say things were going better, but several problems still made him feel like he wasn't doing enough.

He felt better after talking to Oam the other day. They'd had lunch together every day since then, and Tito loved it. He'd usually spent his days with Killian, which he didn't mind. In fact, he liked it. Killian wouldn't be his best friend if they weren't close, and Tito had never thought much of them being together most of the time.

But Oam was just for Tito, and he offered a different point of view than Killian. Killian wouldn't have known how to comfort Tito when he'd broken down the other day, but Oam had. He'd said all the right things, and Tito had felt less alone.

After cleaning the bathroom sink, he dried his hands and turned toward his nest. The egg was settled into it as if it belonged there, and while initially it hadn't felt like it did, Tito was starting to feel that way. The surprise of becoming a father was fading, replaced by heavy responsibilities. Tito would be responsible for a life. He'd have to raise this child to the best of his ability and learn from his mistakes. Thankfully, he wouldn't be doing any of it alone. Oam was right. Tito had him, but also Killian and his family. As long as Tito didn't push them away, he could do this.

A knock on his front door made him frown. He'd taken the morning off. He'd been neglecting his personal life since Killian had taken over the clan and the war had started, and his rooms were a bit of a mess. He could have asked someone to clean them for him, but they were Tito's responsibility, and he wouldn't hand them over to anyone, just like he wouldn't do so with the egg. He'd been puttering around his suite, cleaning up and putting everything to rights. He hoped that whoever was at the door wasn't here to stay because he wasn't quite done yet.

He left the egg in the bedroom and went to open the door. Thankfully, he was used to schooling his expression, because he didn't want his mother to think he wasn't happy to see her. He was.

Mostly.

He stepped aside to let her in. "I didn't expect you. Or did we have an appointment I forgot about?"

She smiled and glanced around the living area. Tito had no doubt she was looking for the egg.

"We didn't have an appointment," she said. "I just wanted to check on you."

"Did you?"

Her eyes narrowed. "Aren't I allowed to check on my son?"

Tito grinned at her. "It's a bit out of character, but we can act as if it isn't."

Tito's mother stared at him for a moment. It always made him want to wriggle, but he forced himself to stay still. He couldn't help but wonder what she saw, though.

After a few moments, she nodded. "You look better. Lighter."

"Well, I feel that way. The war is over, and Killian will be home soon."

"I understand how that would make you feel relieved." She bit her lower lip and looked around again. "It's good to see you happier. I don't want to ruin this."

Tito didn't like the sound of that. "How would you ruin it? What's happening?"

Tito couldn't help but think about the worst possibilities.

Had Delia's parents decided they wanted the egg, after all? Tito wouldn't berate them for it. In fact, he'd understand why they'd changed their mind.

He was getting used to the idea of being a father, and even though the egg hadn't hatched yet, the child already felt like his. It would tear his heart out to have to hand the baby over, but for his aunt and uncle, he'd do it. It would be their right to raise their grandchild.

"The last time I saw you, you weren't doing so good," his mother explained. "So I've been thinking. You have a lot of responsibilities as the king's assistant, and I'm sure you'll have a lot of work in the near future, what with the war and everything the Saganto clan did. I don't want you to have to split your attention between two important things, so I thought it would be better if you gave the egg to me."

It wasn't what Tito had expected, but he wasn't entirely surprised since it wasn't the first time she'd offered to do it. "You talked to Delia's parents?" Maybe they'd asked her to talk to Tito.

"I have, but they confirmed they're happy with how things are now. They want to be grandparents to this child but can't be parents again. They said it would hurt too much, and I understand that. I know you've been in a lot of pain because of what happened to Delia. The two of you were close as children. That's why I thought I could take the child. That way, you won't have to worry about them."

Tito was relieved that he'd left the egg in his bedroom. He didn't expect his mother to try to steal it, but it felt safer to have it there. "I already told you that I don't need you to take on the responsibility."

"You don't need me to do it, but maybe it would be for the best."

"For whom?"

Tito's mother put her hands on her hips. "Both you and the

child. You wouldn't have to split your attention between the child and your job, and you'd have time to relax. The baby would have a parent entirely dedicated to them. I'm not saying you wouldn't be a good father, just that it might be a better idea not to become one."

"I already told you how I felt about that." Tito told himself not to be angry. His mother was doing this because she wanted the best for him and the egg, no matter how angry her suggestion made him. Her heart was in the right place, and she wasn't going to steal the egg. She was just offering an alternative.

Tito needed her to understand he didn't want it.

"Thank you for your offer," he said. "But my answer is still no. Delia wanted me to raise her child, and I will. It doesn't matter if I have to quit my job as Killian's assistant. If that's what I need to do to be a good father, I'll do it."

"You can't quit your job. You're the king's assistant."

Tito shook his head. "I'm not planning to quit. I don't think Killian would allow me to. I'm just telling you what I'm ready to do as a father. I'd quit my job if I had to. Luckily, Killian is my friend, and he knows what I'm going through. He'll give me as much time and space as I need. Hell, he'll even help me raise this child if I asked him to. There's no need for you to worry. I might be a bit overwhelmed at the moment, but that's only because of the war. Now that it's over, everything will be fine."

Tito hoped his mother would believe the massive lie. He didn't, but he was the only one aware of how much trouble the clan was still in.

Oam finished straightening his nest and looked around his room. There wasn't much to it, but he took pride in keeping it as clean and neat as he could. He didn't have servants who would do it for him, but he didn't need them. He enjoyed cleaning, especially when he put music on. It was an activity that didn't force him to think too hard, meaning he could relax.

He checked the time. Even though Tito had taken the morning off, he'd asked Oam if they could have lunch together. They'd been doing so for several days, and even though Oam would never admit it to anyone, he enjoyed it.

He didn't know what he and Tito were doing. They were becoming friends, but sometimes there was something in the way Tito looked at Oam that made him wonder if there was more to it. He wanted to ask, but at the same time, he was terrified of finding out.

He didn't need to. For now, he was fine not knowing what was happening. He was happy as long as he could continue having lunch with Tito and spending time with him.

Luckily, he didn't have a lot of time left before he needed to leave. He was done cleaning, and being idle always messed with his mind. When he had time to think, he started obsessing over what Rutger's mother was plotting, and that wasn't something he wanted to deal with right now.

After washing up, he grabbed the carrier and hooked it around his chest. He extracted the egg from the nest and slid it into the carrier, making sure it was secured. He always did when he left his rooms. He didn't expect anyone to snatch the egg from the carrier, but just in case, he wanted to be prepared.

He and Tito were meeting at the dining hall today. It was the first time they weren't having lunch in Tito's office, and it made Oam a bit nervous. Everyone would see them together, and gossip would start flying.

He didn't care much about what people said about him, but Tito might. After all, he was the king's personal assistant. He probably didn't want people to talk about him and who he had lunch with and to assume there was more between him and Oam than a new friendship.

But Tito had been the one to suggest they eat in the dining hall, and Oam hadn't been able to say no. He hoped Filicia wouldn't find out and that if she did, she'd stay away, but what would be the odds?

He got more and more nervous as he got closer to the dining hall. He wanted to call Tito and ask where he was, but he didn't want Tito to think he was clingy, so instead, he raised his chin high and walked into the hall as if he belonged there.

He did. Everyone in the clan could eat in there. The palace cooks made sure there was enough food for whoever needed it, and while it wasn't a requirement and people could eat in the comfort of their own rooms, everyone had a place here.

Oam looked around, hoping to see people he knew. He noticed a few friends, so he knew he'd have support in case something happened. He hoped Rutger's mother wouldn't be stupid enough to come at Oam in front of so many people, but he wouldn't put it past her.

He quickly grabbed food and found an empty table close to a window. He didn't want to start eating without Tito, but luckily, he could see him in the line waiting to get a plate, so he wouldn't have to wait long.

As soon as Tito was at the end of the line, Oam waved to get his attention. Tito smiled when he saw him, making Oam's stomach churn.

He shouldn't feel so excited at the thought of eating with Tito and even more at the thought that Tito was happy to see him, but he didn't know how to stop this reaction. He wasn't sure he wanted to. Even though he knew nothing would happen, having a crush made him feel normal.

Tito carried his tray to Oam's table. He sat and unhooked the carrier from his chest before gently placing it on the table. Oam quickly did the same because eating with the egg strapped to his chest would be awkward, but now, his stomach churned for an entirely different reason. It would be easy for anyone to walk past their table and snatch the egg.

"How was your morning?" Tito asked as he grabbed his fork.

He couldn't see that Oam was anxious, and Oam wanted to keep things that way.

Oam cleared his throat. "It was fine. What about you? What did you do with your free morning?"

Tito huffed. "My mother came by. She offered to take the egg again."

Oam knew that was a sore point for Tito, so he wasn't surprised when the other dragon started stabbing his food. "She probably just wants to help," he offered.

Tito sighed. "I know, and I even understand why. I won't deny that considering the job I do, it won't be easy for me to raise a child, especially on my own, but it doesn't mean I'm not capable of doing it, and it certainly doesn't mean I'm going to give up the baby. I already told my mother that, and I wish she'd listen to me instead of assuming what I want or what would be better."

Oam could understand some of that. His mother had been concerned when he'd decided to take his egg. It had nothing to do with his job but rather with how the egg had been created. She didn't get that when Oam looked at his child, he didn't see Rutger. He only saw himself and the future he and his baby would have, and he desperately wanted it to happen. That was why he would fight anyone who tried to take his child from him, no matter how powerful or influential they were.

Tito had his back to the room, so he didn't see Rutger's mother coming toward them. Oam did, though, and he dropped his fork. His brain felt frozen, but his hands weren't. He grabbed the carrier and hooked it around his body, then, for good measure, he wrapped his arms around the egg.

"What's wrong?" Tito asked, frowning.

Oam didn't have time to answer. Filicia had reached them.

"You should be ashamed of yourself," she snapped. "How can you do this to me?"

Tito frowned and started to turn, but Oam shook his head. He didn't want Rutger's mother to see who he was having lunch with. "I'm not doing anything to you. I'm eating lunch."

"You're flaunting the fact that you stole my son's egg. You have it there, and knowing you, you're only here because you wanted me to see it and be hurt."

Oam's mouth was dry. "I never wanted to hurt you, but this is my child, not yours. Considering how I got pregnant, I won't allow you anywhere near my child. You supported your son, and it's not something I can forgive."

He still didn't know why Rutger had chosen him and didn't care what the dragon had seen in him. He just knew that Rutger had been a guard to King Eldar. When he'd decided he wanted Oam, and Oam had said no because he couldn't imagine anyone worse to have a child with, Rutger had gone to the king. He'd asked for Oam, and the king hadn't hesitated to hand him over. Rutger's family had supported him. Hell, Oam remembered how excited they'd been that Rutger would have a child. Rutger was close to the king, so they'd expected Eldar to allow him and his family to raise the child.

But they wouldn't. Rutger was dead, and Oam had taken his egg back. He wouldn't allow Filicia anywhere near it. He'd fight her if he had to.

Tito gritted his teeth. Oam didn't want him to intervene, but how could he ignore what this dragon was saying? They were mean and hurting Oam, and that wasn't something Tito could allow, especially considering what they were saying.

He didn't have all the information about how Oam had gotten pregnant, but he could imagine how it happened all too well. Before Killian took his father's place on the throne, the law had been that anyone who was fertile had to have a child. If they couldn't find someone to have the child with, someone would be chosen for them. Usually, that someone was the king or someone close to him. In this case, it sounded like whoever had forced Oam into this had gone to the king and asked for him.

And the dragon's family hadn't done anything to stop it from happening.

Tito understood not wanting to get the king's attention because it could have led to imprisonment, but that wasn't what had happened here. It sounded like the dragon talking to Oam had wanted their son to have a child and didn't care what Oam thought or felt. It wasn't like this dragon hadn't tried to protect Oam because they were afraid they'd end up in jail. No, they hadn't done anything because they'd wanted it to happen. They hadn't cared what Oam wanted, and it sounded like they still didn't.

Tito hated how Oam was shrinking into himself, as if he were trying to disappear. People around them were starting to notice something was happening, and they were turning to get a better look. This dragon was making a scene, and Tito couldn't stand that.

He saw the panic in Oam's eyes when he turned, and while he wished he could do what Oam wanted, he wouldn't allow anyone to hurt him like this dragon was.

"Just leave me alone," Oam quickly said. "Please. I never wanted any of this to happen, but I couldn't stop it. I'm trying to do the best with what I have, and I don't want to fight with anyone."

The dragon stepped closer to the table. "If you didn't want

to fight with me, you should have given me the egg. I don't care what you want, Oam. That baby is *mine*."

Tito didn't stand up, but he didn't have to. He turned to face the dragon and saw the moment they realized who he was. They paled and took a step back, but they didn't leave, allowing Tito to examine them.

He was pretty sure this dragon was a female from her jewelry. Her hair was long and neatly tied up. Tito couldn't tell how old she was, but it was always hard with dragons. Her pale orange color was pretty, but now that Tito had heard what she had to say, he knew she was a monster inside.

"Who is this person?" Tito asked Oam.

Oam looked like he was seriously considering hiding under the table. He was clinging to his egg, and the fear in his eyes went straight to Tito's heart. How could anyone hurt Oam? He was sweet and hadn't done anything to deserve any of this. He hadn't been allowed to choose when he wanted a child or who he wanted it with, and he was dealing with what life had given him and what Eldar had forced onto him the best he could. Tito wouldn't allow anyone to hurt him ever again.

Beginning with this dragon.

"My name is Filicia," the dragon said as she quickly bowed.

Tito almost rolled his eyes. He wasn't Killian, but many dragons saw him as an extension of him. That couldn't have been further from the truth. He and Killian were friends, but they were two separate people, and Tito didn't need to be bowed to.

To be fair, neither did Killian, but he couldn't say anything about it because he was the king. Tito had no such compulsions, and usually, he told the people he was with not to treat him as if he were part of the royal family.

He wasn't about to tell Filicia that. In fact, he *wanted* her to treat him as if he were Killian. Maybe she'd respect him and leave Oam alone.

"I'd say it's a pleasure to meet you, but it isn't," Tito drawled.

Oam's eyes went wide, and Tito could see he wanted to say something, but he didn't. He stayed as still as possible, as if he was afraid that if he moved, Filicia would see him and strike.

"I apologize for what you had to hear," Filicia said. "I'm just trying to do the best for my grandchild."

"And you think the best is making a scene in the middle of the dining hall?"

Her skin was pale, so when she flushed, it was obvious. Her cheeks and chest turned pink, and the patches of pale orange scales darkened. Tito noticed her gritting her teeth. He was pretty sure she hated him, even though he'd never met her before. He suspected she hated a lot of people, and for some reason, one of those people was Oam.

Tito didn't understand how anyone could hate Oam, but he didn't know much about this situation. He had suspicions, and he wasn't sure he'd be able to get more details because it was clear Oam didn't want to talk about it, but maybe it would be necessary. The last thing Tito wanted was to hurt Oam, but he might have to if it meant keeping Filicia away.

"I apologize for this," Filicia said. "But I'm sure you can understand. I'm distraught, and I wasn't thinking. Oam has been keeping my grandchild from me, and after so recently losing my son, it's not easy to deal with."

"That still doesn't explain why you thought yelling at him would be a good idea. To be honest, I don't care why you did it. I just need you to stop."

She bowed again. "Of course. I apologize."

She glared at Oam, but thankfully, she didn't say anything else to him before leaving.

Most of the people in the dining hall had been staring, but they quickly looked away when Tito arched a brow. Gossip would fly, both because of what had just happened and because people would wonder why Tito was sitting with Oam.

People could assume what they wanted. As long as Oam was all right, Tito didn't care.

He turned to Oam. "Are you all right?"

Oam was pale, but he relaxed as if he trusted Tito to protect him.

He could. Tito didn't know when it had happened, but Oam had become important to him.

"I'm sorry you had to see that," Oam murmured. "I knew she might be in the dining hall, but I hoped she'd let me eat in peace. I didn't think she wouldn't see you or that she wouldn't hesitate to confront me in front of so many people."

"You have nothing to apologize for. You're not responsible for her behavior or for what she said. I don't want you to worry about it, all right?"

"I'll try, but it's hard not to."

Tito wished he could do more for Oam, and maybe he could, but he needed the entire story first, and he didn't think Oam was ready to give it to him.

For a moment, they were both silent. Tito went back to his food and waited for Oam to do the same. He wouldn't have been surprised if Oam couldn't eat anymore, but after poking at his food for a moment, he did. It helped that the people around them weren't focused on them anymore.

"What were you saying about your mother?" Oam eventually asked.

Clearly, he didn't want to talk about Filicia, and for now, Tito would allow it. He didn't want to talk about his mother, but he would if it meant distracting Oam. "She makes me angry, even though she means well."

Oam nodded. "I get it."

Tito allowed Oam this distraction, but at the back of his mind, he was already making a list of what he needed to know about Oam's situation. He didn't want to intrude on Oam's privacy, but if he was going to protect Oam from Filicia, he'd need to find out what was going on. If Oam didn't want to tell him, Tito would have to find a way around that.

But he might lose Oam if he did so, and he wasn't ready for that to happen.

CHAPTER SEVEN

K illian was coming home.

Tito had known it for several days, but it felt like it hadn't been long enough for him to do everything he had to get the clan ready for the king. He'd had to organize a welcome home party, and Killian would have to address the entire clan, which meant a public announcement. Security had to be beefed up because Marlin and Birch would be exhausted, but Tito didn't have many guards left, so he didn't know where to get them. The fact that Killian had decided to take in some of the refugees from the clans that the Saganto clan had destroyed also didn't help. They had more clan members than ever, and while these people were settling in, it was still a lot of work for them to heal and become productive after what had happened to them.

The renovations of the palace were still ongoing, so part of it was closed off, which meant less space to celebrate. With the influx of new members, things were getting a little tight, which was something else Tito had to take care of. He also had to keep up with the cooks and the cleaners, and of course, he couldn't ignore the problems the clan had that he would have to tell Killian about soon.

Then, there was Oam.

He hadn't been avoiding Tito, but they hadn't seen each other much. Tito had initially been careful not to talk about Filicia and what had happened in the dining hall. After Killian had declared he was coming home, he didn't have to be careful anymore because he barely had the time to eat and sleep, let alone talk to Oam. He wanted to ask about his child and what had happened, but it would have to wait until Killian was back and the celebration was over. Since Tito couldn't spend time with Oam, it meant he couldn't ensure that Filicia left him alone.

Sometimes, he wished his days had forty-eight hours instead of twenty-four. He suspected that even then, they wouldn't be long enough to do everything on his lists, but maybe he'd be able to relax just a bit more.

Samsa barged into the office, almost falling on her face. She caught herself on a chair and turned wide eyes to Tito. "They're here."

Tito jumped to his feet. He had the egg strapped to his chest because he'd known that when Killian was close, he'd have to run to the landing area. He hadn't wanted anything to slow him down, so even though working with the egg on his chest had been awkward, he'd felt it was the best way to go about it. It meant he could run out of his office without delay.

Samsa was behind him. He heard her slip in her haste to keep up with him, but beyond checking that she hadn't hurt herself, he didn't slow down. He wanted to be one of the first to greet Killian when he landed, and he didn't care if people thought it was ridiculous or that it wasn't his place. Killian was his best friend, and he'd been terrified he'd lose him. He had the right to hug the stuffing out of him, dammit.

Tito was out of breath when he reached the landing area. The day was clear, which meant he could see the approaching dragons when he looked up at the sky. He came to stand next to Killian's mother. She looked regal, not out of breath like Tito. He was pretty sure his hair was a mess, too, so he quickly tried to smooth it down.

"I thought you'd be late," the queen murmured.

"I was working."

"What's so important that you had to work when you knew Killian was coming back?" She glanced Tito's way. "Are we in trouble?"

"Nothing you have to worry about right now," he promised.

He wasn't lying. The Eiloren clan had a massive money problem, but there was nothing the queen could do about it today. Hell, there was nothing *anyone* could do. There would be time to tell Killian tomorrow after he had time to celebrate and rest.

Instead of running forward as he wanted as soon as Killian touched the ground, Tito turned to Killian's mother. He knew how much she wanted to hug her son, and he wouldn't take that from her.

But instead of moving forward, she grabbed Tito's shoulder and pushed him. "Go. I can't make a scene because of who I am, but you don't care."

Damn right, Tito didn't. He didn't care what the people watching thought of him. Whatever it was, it wouldn't change the fact that he was Killian's best friend and that Killian loved and respected him. It also wouldn't change the fact that Tito had missed Killian and that he'd been terrified he'd never see his friend again, so he rushed forward.

Killian shifted to his human form and laughed. When he opened his arms, Tito stepped into them. Because of the egg, he had to be careful, but Killian's strong arms wrapped around him and squeezed. Tito breathed easier.

Killian was home. Everything would be all right.

"I take it you missed me?" Killian teased as he let go of Tito.

Tito glared at him, but there was no heat in it. "Things have been so peaceful without you. Why would I have missed you?"

Killian laughed again and wrapped an arm around Tito's shoulder. "Whatever you say. How's your kid?"

It touched Tito that Killian saw the baby as his. It was more than he could say for a lot of people. "They're fine. How was the trip?"

"I have so many things to tell you," Killian said, but he didn't have the time to explain.

They'd reached his mother, and he let go of Tito to hug her.

Tito kept a respectful distance for a little while so Killian had the space to greet the people who were there to see him, but he didn't stray too far in case Killian disappeared on him.

Eventually, they reached Killian's office. Killian flopped onto one of the couches by the window and gestured at Tito to close the door. Tito glanced out and nodded at Marlin and Birch. "Go wash up and get some rest. We'll be in the office for a little while."

Tito knew they'd be back soon. They took their job of protecting the king seriously. Tito was glad because it meant he didn't have to worry too much about Killian and what he was up to. Even when he was an idiot, he was protected.

He closed the door and sucked in a breath. With Killian here, it felt like everything was back to normal.

Killian sprawled on the couch. "Well? Tell me what happened while I was gone."

Tito was sure that Killian meant for him to explain what happened to the clan calmly, but instead, a torrent of words poured from his lips.

"I met someone. His name is Oam, and he became a father recently. His egg hasn't hatched yet, but you know what I mean. I don't know much about how he became pregnant, but it wasn't a happy time, as you can imagine considering the laws your father had put in place. Oam is doing the best he can, even though the mother of the child's second father is being an asshole and hounding him. There's also the fact that my mother seems to think I'm incapable of raising a child and being your personal assistant at the same time, and of course, the many problems with the refugees, the renovation of the palace, and the fact that we have approximately zero money left to take care of all of that. Organizing the party was a stretch, and I don't know how the clan will survive if you don't find money somewhere."

Tito sucked in a breath. He was horrified at what had come out of his mouth, but there was nothing he could do to take the words back. Killian appeared as shocked as Tito felt, blinking a few times as he stared at him.

Tito groaned and sat on the couch in front of Killian. He rubbed his face and tried to find the right words this time. "I'm sorry."

Killian leaned forward. "What are you sorry for? You had this weight on your shoulders and couldn't deal with it anymore. It's fine, Tito. I'm home. The Saganto clan's wealth will be divided between all the clans that fought against them, and from what I know, it's a lot of money. You can relax."

Tito wished he was right, but he was afraid to hope.

Everyone in the clan was excited because the king was home. Oam was, too, but while he was glad the war was over and that the king was back, he was even happier because it meant that Tito had his best friend back.

No one knew how worried Tito had been when he had to leave Killian with the Ogorth clan and come home. He hadn't wanted to, but he'd felt his duty as a new father was to protect his child and take them as far away as possible from the war. Choosing between the child and his best friend had to have been hard, but Tito had done it, and Oam didn't think he regretted it. Having him here meant that Tito could relax now.

He and Killian would have a lot of work to do. Oam had given Tito space because he'd known Tito would be focused on his work. He didn't need Oam adding to it, even though

Oam wanted nothing more than to talk to him. He'd missed Tito more than he'd expected.

A knock on his door brought him out of his thoughts. Like always, he hesitated to open, but his mom was supposed to come over so they could walk to the celebration party together.

He picked up his phone from the nightstand and called his mother, relieved when he heard her phone ring on the other side of his door.

He opened the door and caught her as she took out her phone. She slipped it back into the pouch around her neck and grabbed Oam to hug him. The egg wasn't strapped to his chest yet, so she could do so without anything separating them.

"You look handsome tonight," she said.

Oam hadn't been sure he should attend the party. He wanted to, but he feared Filicia and what she'd do if she saw him there. Tito had asked him to come, though, and Oam couldn't say no. If Tito wanted him there, he'd be there. Hopefully, Filicia would ignore him like she had since Tito had talked to her in the dining hall.

Since Oam would be seeing Tito tonight, he'd put some effort into his appearance. He wore makeup and a few pieces of jewelry, but he'd tried not to go overboard. He didn't want to look ridiculous, but he did want Tito to notice him.

"Well, it's a party," he told his mother as he went back into his room to grab the carrier and hook it around his chest.

"And maybe there's someone special you want to impress tonight."

"Tito is a friend, nothing more."

"For now. You do have a crush on him, though."

Oam hadn't told his mother, but she knew him better than he knew himself sometimes. "Maybe I do have a crush on Tito, but nothing will happen. We both have enough things to worry about without adding a relationship to it."

"Don't think like that. No matter how busy the two of you are, you need to make time to have a private life and have fun. You like Tito, and I'm sure he likes you. What better moment for you to get together than a party?"

Oam didn't want to disappoint his mother. Besides, he *did* wish that he and Tito would get together. He liked Tito, and it went beyond the fact that Tito had stood up for him in the dining hall.

A lot of the time, Tito acted as if he hated his job and the problems he had to deal with, but Oam suspected that if he were to quit, he'd miss it. Deep inside, he enjoyed solving problems and ensuring everything was as it should be. He had a strong sense of right and wrong, which was why he'd helped Killian obtain the throne. He'd had to rise against the king to do so, which couldn't have been easy, but he had.

Tito never hesitated to tell people what he thought of the way they behaved, but he was also lovely and sweet. He didn't take bullshit from anyone, and he was always ready to help. He made Oam feel protected, which meant more than anything else to Oam. He could be himself with Tito because he knew he was safe.

He didn't want to hope too much, though. He didn't know what would happen during the party, but Tito would be busy. Still, as he and his mother walked toward the throne room, Oam couldn't help but check his reflection in every window they walked past. He wanted Tito to think he was handsome.

The throne room was already overrun with people. Oam clung to his egg and stuck close to his mother, relieved when they joined the rest of their family. They instantly moved around him to form a protective circle. They might still be hesitant about Oam keeping his child, but it was what Oam wanted, and they supported him. He hadn't had a choice in most of what had happened, but keeping his child *was* his choice, and his family respected that.

The level of noise in the room rose when the king arrived. Oam tried to get a good look. The area on which the throne was set was higher than the rest of the room, but with so many people around him, it was hard.

The room fell silent, and everyone stilled. Killian stepped forward, stopping in front of the throne and looking down at the people gathered to celebrate his return. Oam held his breath. He had a good idea of what the king would say but was still emotional. They'd stood to lose their clan and everything they had. They would have if the Saganto clan hadn't been defeated.

"We won the war," Killian declared. His voice was strong and echoed around the room.

It sounded like every single dragon in the throne room cheered at the same time. It was loud, but it brought tears to Oam's eyes.

Killian raised his hands. "The Saganto clan is gone. They'll never threaten anyone again. We are safe from them, and it's time for us to celebrate that. I won't lie and tell you that everything will be perfect from now on. There are many things we'll need to deal with, and life might be hard for a while longer, but the danger is gone. It's time for us to heal."

Oam suspected Killian wasn't just talking about the Saganto clan. His father was gone, which meant the clan was free of him. Unfortunately, what Eldar had done to the clan was worse than what the Saganto clan had done to them during the war, and they'd have to heal from that, too.

But with the Saganto clan gone, they'd have the opportunity to do so. *That* was what was important.

Everyone cheered again, and music started playing. People drifted toward the long tables set around the throne room to get food. Oam should probably do the same, but he'd rather keep his distance for now. He didn't want his family to avoid the celebrations to be with him, so after promising he'd be careful, he moved toward a corner of the room. Here, he could keep an eye on the party and enjoy himself while not being overwhelmed by the crowd. As a bonus, he'd be able to notice if someone came toward him.

He hated that he always had to be careful, but until the situation with Filicia was resolved, he didn't have a choice.

Tito was tense as he kept an eye on the crowd. Marlin and Birch stood close to Killian, who thankfully was still by the throne. That meant that most of the clan members partying around them couldn't reach him, but it didn't mean someone wouldn't try. The bodyguards would step in if anyone did, but Tito hoped it wouldn't come to that.

"You know this is a party," Killian teased.

"I'm aware of that. I wouldn't be wearing jewelry if it weren't."

"You look good tonight. Is it because you have someone to impress?"

Tito narrowed his eyes. "Remind me why I'm friends with you again?"

"Because I'm irresistible. Seriously, though. Where's your man?"

Tito looked around. There were so many people that finding Oam in the crowd felt impossible. He could call him, but he knew Oam well by now. He felt he could predict what Oam would do in this situation.

Oam didn't like crowds. More importantly, he'd be carrying the egg. That meant he'd want a quiet place where no one would bump into him, but also that he'd want to be able to see anyone coming toward him. He hadn't given Tito details, but there was no doubt in Tito's mind that Oam wanted to avoid Filicia as much as he could. Hell, Tito wanted to avoid her, and he'd only talked to her once.

Tito let his gaze skip the tables where the crowd had gathered to get food and drinks and rove over the quieter spaces in the room. He found Oam in a corner, keeping an eye on the crowd.

"There he is," he said, leaning closer to Killian.

Killian looked in the direction Tito was indicating. He grinned when he found Oam. It wasn't hard to identify him, since he was clutching his egg. "He's cute."

"And he's mine," Tito warned.

Killian grinned and raised his hands. "I wasn't thinking about taking him from you. I'd never do that." He leaned closer. "You should go to him."

"I think I'll bring him here instead, if that's okay with you." Tito wasn't sure Oam would like that because people were bound to notice, but it would be better than if Tito joined Oam in the crowd. People would see them together either way, but if they were close to Killian, Oam would be better protected.

Tito didn't know a lot about Filicia, but he wouldn't put it past her to try to hurt Oam tonight. She didn't need to attack him to hurt him. A few well-placed words would be enough.

Killian waved at Birch to come closer. When he did, he pointed at Oam. "Can you bring him here?"

Birch arched a brow and looked at Tito as if he expected him to give another order. Killian rolled his eyes and glared while Tito nodded. Birch didn't waste any more time and turned to leave.

"It's not fair," Killian complained. "I'm the king. Why doesn't he obey my orders without checking with you first?"

"He probably understands that you're really a kid playing with the crown."

"Most of the time, I wish I were."

Killian hadn't taken the throne with a light heart. Tito wouldn't say he hadn't wanted to become king, but he definitely hadn't wanted to become king in the way it had happened. Killian had been raised to take his father's place one day, and he'd always known the crown would be his. What he hadn't expected was to have to kick his father off the throne because the dragon had gone nuts.

Tito didn't think that was what happened. Killian's father had allowed the power to go to his head. He'd thought himself a god rather than a king, controlling when people should have children and who they should have them with. He'd used the clan's wealth for his own benefit, and now the clan was in trouble.

But that wasn't something Tito wanted to think about tonight. Killian knew everything there was to know about the clan's problems, and he'd promised they'd get through it. He wasn't one to make empty promises, especially to Tito, so Tito believed him. They could relax and celebrate the end of the war for tonight, and tomorrow, they'd deal with the problems left behind by Killian's father and the Saganto clan.

Birch finally reached Oam, which pulled Tito's attention away from Killian. He watched as Birch leaned closer to talk to Oam, and Oam's eyes widened. Oam looked up, his gaze latching onto Tito.

Tito smiled and nodded at him. Oam visibly relaxed, as if he'd expected Birch to have been sent by someone else. Tito didn't have to wonder who that was.

Filicia was another problem Tito would have to deal with, and he didn't think it could wait. She wanted Oam's baby, and the other day, it had felt like she'd do anything in her power to get them. Oam would fight her, but he might not be able to do much to stop her.

Tito could.

He didn't like using his influence as Killian's best friend, but he would if he had to. He didn't care what people thought of him doing so. He didn't want people to bow to him just because he happened to be the king's friend, but he wouldn't hesitate to use his power to stop Filicia from taking Oam's child from him. She had no right to do so, even though she was the child's grandmother.

Birch cut a path through the crowd. He kept an eye on Oam, who was right behind him. As soon as they were close enough to the throne pedestal, Birch stepped aside and let Oam climb the stairs before him. He quickly followed him, glaring at someone who tried to do the same.

Luckily, the clan was well-behaved. People were trying to get Killian's attention, but they weren't rushing him or trying to climb the pedestal, apart from a few exceptions who were quickly dealt with. They were giving him space to celebrate, have fun, and hopefully relax.

It wouldn't last long for either of them.

Oam made a beeline for Tito. He was visibly out of his depth but hadn't resisted the summoning. Tito didn't want to make him uncomfortable, but he felt better now that Oam was with him.

Of course, that was the moment Killian chose to focus on Tito again. His eyes lit up when he saw that Oam had joined them, and he stepped closer. Oam looked startled by the king's attention and tried to move away, but there wasn't much space, and his back hit the throne. He paled so quickly that Tito wondered if he was about to faint.

"I'm sorry about that," he said.

Killian waved his words away. "Don't worry. It was my father's throne, and I have no love for it. I haven't burnt it yet because Tito warned me of how much money it would cost to get a new one."

Oam looked at Tito as if asking for confirmation. Tito rolled his eyes. "He's not lying. He did want to burn it down. I'm sure you can imagine he has no love for anything his father did."

Oam's gaze softened. "It's good to have you back, your Majesty."

"That won't do," Killian declared. "I want you to call me Killian."

And there was the panic again. It was clear in Oam's expression. Tito wanted to smack Killian for scaring Oam, but at the same time, he wanted Oam and Killian to be comfortable with each other. If Oam was going to be in Tito's life — and Tito hoped he would be — he had to get used to spending time with Killian and see him as the dragon he was rather than as the king.

"He does want you to call him Killian," Tito confirmed. "Just try to ignore he's the king."

"I don't know if I can do that."

"It'll get easier as you get to know me," Killian promised. "Now, why don't you tell me about your egg. I'm sure you know that Tito has one, too. Will you be raising the children as siblings?"

Tito groaned. He'd been wary of having Killian and Oam meet, and now he knew he'd been right. Killian was teasing, but Oam didn't know him well enough to realize that.

Oh, well. Tito wanted Oam to learn how to deal with Killian, and he supposed that now was as good as any moment. Everyone was relaxed and happy, and while Tito could see people staring at Oam, he suspected a lot of them wouldn't remember half of what happened tonight by tomorrow morning. Tito had been careful when he'd planned the party because of the clan's money troubles, but luckily, there had been plenty of wine and alcohol in the palace's reserves.

And from the looks of it, the clan had decided to drink all of it.

CHAPTER EIGHT

K illian's office had three doors. One opened into the throne room, one into Tito's office, and the other into Samsa's. When the door between Killian and Tito's office opened, Tito looked up and watched the dragon in charge of the teams that cleaned the palace step out. "Everyone is so happy you're back and that the war is over," she told Killian.

"I imagine it's something everyone is happy about. The Saganto clan was a great threat, but they're gone."

Eliana bowed lightly. Killian grimaced, but thankfully, she didn't see it. Only Tito did, and he narrowed his eyes at his friend. He wasn't about to scold him in front of Eliana, but Killian needed to stop behaving like he was just another dragon.

Technically, he was, and Tito would never treat him as anything other than a friend, but to most of the dragons in the clan, he was the king. He needed to behave as such, which meant not rolling his eyes when people bowed at him.

Tito already knew that no matter how many times he brought it up, Killian would ignore him. He was infuriatingly stubborn, and if Tito hadn't loved him so much, he would already have given up on him a long time ago.

Eliana turned to Tito. Her gaze stopped on the egg he kept on the couch by the window. She smiled, and even though Tito barely knew her, he found himself doing the same. That was what babies did. They made people happy.

"Congratulations on becoming a father," she told Tito.

"Thank you." What else was he supposed to say?

"And I'm very sorry for your loss. I remember your cousin when she was a child. The two of you played in the hallways even when you shouldn't have and got in all kinds of trouble."

Sometimes, Tito hated that everyone in the clan had known him when he was a child. He was supposed to have authority over these people, but instead, they remembered when he'd thrown up because he'd eaten too much sugar and when he'd broken a vase in the dining hall.

In Tito's defense, why had anyone been keeping fragile objects in the dining hall, of all places?

"Well, it won't be long now. It'll be a pleasure to have another baby in the palace," she continued.

Tito nodded, but his attention was on the egg. He barely noticed when Eliana left or that Killian had gone back to his office. He was thinking about what would come next and how much trouble babies and children could get into.

For now, it was easy to bring the egg to work. Tito just had to put it on the couch, and it wouldn't move. It needed to be kept warm, but it didn't cry and didn't need to be fed or cleaned.

That would change when the egg hatched. How was Tito going to deal with it then? Bringing a baby dragon to work sounded horrible, and not just for Tito. There was nothing to amuse a child here, and they'd get into trouble. Besides, it didn't feel fair. When Tito was with the child, he wanted to focus on them, not work.

He startled himself at the realization. Just a few weeks ago, he would never have thought that taking time away from work sounded good. Hell, the thought of stepping away from this job, even temporarily, would have given him hives. He could imagine all too well the kind of trouble Killian would get himself into if Tito wasn't there to keep an eye on him.

But the baby had changed everything. It had made Tito

aware of how much time he spent at work, even when it wasn't necessary. He hadn't taken time off since Killian had become king, but he wondered if he could get Killian to give him a few days when the egg hatched. Killian would probably force him to take a few *weeks*, but Tito didn't want to be away for that long. He just wanted a good balance of work and personal life. His job was too important to stay away for long, but maybe he could find a way to make everything work together.

It would be easy to ask Tito's mother if she could keep the baby when he was working. She'd probably jump on the opportunity, and it was understandable. Technically, the baby was her first grandchild. Tito wanted her to be in the baby's life, but part of him was reluctant to ask her for help. She'd tried to convince him to give up the egg a few times. Even though she meant well, it felt like a betrayal and as if she believed he would be incapable of working and taking care of the baby at the same time.

Tito would prove her wrong. He'd prove everyone wrong.

A soft knock on the door made him look up. He expected Samsa, but instead, Oam peeked in.

Tito frowned and checked the time. "How is it already so late?" he asked as he realized it was time for lunch.

"We can skip lunch today if you have too much work to do," Oam offered.

Tito waved him in. "We're not skipping anything. Having lunch with you is the only light in an otherwise dark day, and I need to take a break."

Oam's cheeks flushed as he fully walked into the office. Tito didn't have to tell Samsa to have lunch brought up to them. She was at her desk, so she'd know Oam was here.

Oam and Tito had been having lunch together almost every day, and they had a routine down. Oam went straight for the couches by the window and unhooked his egg from the carrier. He placed it into the small nest Tito had created on the couch, and Tito couldn't look away from the two eggs settled there together.

The eggs were wildly different, but they could have been siblings anyway. There was a hint of blue in the deep magenta of Tito's egg, and while Oam's egg was almost entirely pale blue, there were speckles of deep pink hidden there. Tito didn't know what color the egg's other father had been, and he didn't care. He just knew that the egg was gorgeous, just like Oam.

Oam sat down. "What were you thinking about? You were frowning so hard that I expected you to start yelling at me when I interrupted you."

Tito got up and stretched. "I'd never yell at you. No, I was thinking about what would happen when the egg hatches. It's easy to bring it to work now, but it won't be once I have a baby instead of an egg."

Oam nodded as if he'd already thought of that problem. "I'm lucky I don't have to worry about that. I was given time off work, so I'll be able to focus on the baby."

"I could take time off, too, but I'd have to find a solution by the time parental leave is over, anyway. Besides, I don't know if I can take that much time off. Killian will set the palace on fire if I stay away too long."

Oam smiled. "He's not as stupid as you seem to believe he is, you know? I'm sure he can be careful."

Tito flopped onto the couch next to Oam. "You don't know him well yet. I've seen some of the things he did, so pardon me if I'm afraid to leave him alone at the head of the clan."

"You see him in a unique way. You grew up with him, so he shows you things he wouldn't show anyone else. You really should have more faith in him. But I understand why you don't want to step away from your job for too long. Being the king's personal assistant is a big responsibility, and you don't want Killian to have to deal with a subpar assistant or do the job himself."

Tito was glad Oam got it. "Exactly. We've finally settled into our roles, and having someone take my place would be hard. At the same time, I can't keep the baby here after they hatch."

But Oam would be on parental leave. Those tended to be quite long because dragons seldom had children. If Oam wanted, he could stay with his child for a few years and still get his entire salary.

As long as Killian fixed the clan's money problems, anyway.

Tito folded one of his legs and turned to face Oam. "What would you think if I offered to pay you to babysit my child?"

Oam blinked. "What do you mean?"

"Well, you're going to be home with your baby for a while, right? I realize it'll be a lot more work, but there's no one I trust more than you to watch my child. What do you think? Is that something you're willing to consider?"

It surprised Tito to realize that apart from Killian, he truly wouldn't trust anyone else with this baby. He and Oam had grown close since he'd returned from the Ogorth clan palace, and Tito wanted their children to grow up together.

What better way than to have Oam watch them together?

Oam hadn't expected the offer, but he didn't have to think about it. His answer was obvious. "Of course I'll watch your child."

Tito cocked his head. "I expected to have to convince you."

"Why? You're right. I'll be at home with my baby, and while it might get a bit complicated to have to take care of two, I don't mind. It'll be good for them to grow up together."

Tito smiled. "That's what I was thinking."

Oam was happy to say yes, but he was also surprised. Tito

had said there was no one he trusted more with his child than him, and Oam had a hard time wrapping his mind around that. Tito could have asked anyone to watch his child, including his family, but instead, he was asking Oam. He wanted Oam to help raise his child.

All of this was so confusing. Oam had no idea what Tito felt for him. Sometimes, he was sure they were nothing more than friends, but other times, Tito watched him with an intensity that had nothing to do with friendship. He wanted to ask, but he didn't dare. He didn't want to lose Tito's friendship in case he was seeing this all wrong.

"And, of course, I'll pay you," Tito continued.

Oam shook his head. "No. I don't want your money."

"Watching my child is a job. Why wouldn't I pay you?"

"Because we're friends. I don't want you to pay me to do something I'll happily do for free. Even though I'm on parental leave, I still get paid for my job. I'm taken care of, so you don't have to worry about it."

"Killian pays me very well. I can afford it."

Oam rolled his eyes. "Did I say you couldn't afford it? That's not why I don't want your money. I don't need or want it. Watching your child isn't a job to me. It's a pleasure and a favor I'm doing for a friend."

"Maybe so, but raising two children isn't going to be easy. You deserve compensation for it."

Oam could see he wouldn't convince Tito otherwise. They were friends, but Tito wasn't wrong. Watching his child every day and, in a way, raising them, would be a job.

But not if Oam was the child's second parent.

He swallowed. He'd just been thinking that he didn't want things to change between them or to lose Tito's friendship, so this was probably the worst idea he'd ever had, but he needed Tito to understand. He hadn't said yes because he wanted money. He'd said yes because he *wanted* to watch Tito's child.

He wanted to raise their children together as siblings.

Killian had hit the nail right on the head the night of the party. He'd asked if they were going to raise the children as siblings, and while Oam would never have said yes at that point, he'd wanted to. Acting on impulse was nothing like Oam, but he told his brain to shut up for once. He leaned forward and pressed his lips against Tito's, effectively shutting him up while he was still ranting about needing to pay Oam.

His voice cut off instantly. For a moment, neither of them moved. Tito didn't give Oam time to start worrying, though. Seconds after their lips touched, he wrapped his arms around Oam's waist and pulled him closer.

They were sitting side-by-side on the couch, and their positions made the kiss a bit awkward until Tito almost climbed on top of Oam. Oam felt his entire body flush with heat, and when Tito sat in his lap, he grabbed Tito's hips and held him in place.

This had gone from zero to a hundred in record time.

Tito's lips were soft but demanding, just like the dragon himself. He knew what he wanted and wasn't afraid to push until he got it. Oam, on the other hand, was more hesitant. It had been a while since he'd kissed anyone. He hadn't allowed Rutger even to try, which had angered the dragon. Sometimes, Oam thought that Rutger had believed he was in love with Oam, but if he had been, he wouldn't have hurt Oam the way he had.

Oam didn't want to think about Rutger right now. He *never* wanted to think about him.

He tried to put some distance between him and Tito so he could breathe, but Tito seemed intent on not allowing that. He chuckled, and Tito finally let go.

He didn't climb off Oam's lap, though. They stared at each other for a moment. Oam was speechless and trying to make his brain restart, but it was stuck on the fact that Tito was in his lap, and they'd just kissed.

He cleared his throat. "I'll watch your child because I want to and because I like you. I don't need or want you to pay me."

Tito grinned. "I think I got that."

Oam groaned and tried to hide his face with his hands, but Tito would have none of that. He grabbed Oam's wrists and put his hands back on his hips. "We're going to have to talk about this."

"Do we have to do it now?" Oam couldn't think of anything worse. He didn't want to forget that they'd just kissed, but he felt awkward and wasn't ready to talk.

Tito's answering smile was almost feral. "We don't. In fact, I don't believe we should."

Oam frowned. "No?"

"We have something much better to do."

It took Oam a moment to realize what he meant, and when he did, his stomach churned in the best of ways. "I want that, too."

"Good."

Tito leaned forward again, and Oam welcomed him. He had no idea what he was doing or what was happening between them, but maybe he didn't need to know.

He trusted Tito. Tito would never do anything to hurt him, and he'd be honest. He wouldn't try to manipulate Oam, which was a relief. No, Tito would tell Oam what he wanted from him and from their relationship. He'd take all the guesswork out of the situation, which was what Oam needed.

Tito was perfect for him. It sounded cheesy, but they fit together like puzzle pieces. They smoothed each other's angles. Oam didn't know if they were meant to be together, but it kind of felt like they were.

He hoped so.

CHAPTER NINE

Things were going much better than Oam had expected, but then, he hadn't expected Tito to want him the same way he wanted Tito.

He leaned back in his nest and grinned at the ceiling. Even though several days had passed, he still couldn't believe he'd kissed Tito.

He wasn't a spontaneous person. He liked to be comfortable, which meant keeping a familiar routine. When he'd had relationships before, it had always been the other dragon who'd taken the first step.

Not this time. This time, Oam had been brave. He'd kissed Tito even though he hadn't been sure Tito wanted him, and the gamble had paid off. Tito did want him. He'd made that clear and continued doing so every time they saw each other.

Oam's body heated at the memory of the day of their first kiss. Tito's assistant had walked in on them making out on the couch. She'd been bringing in lunch, and while Oam had been flustered and tempted to hide under the coffee table, Tito had acted as if they hadn't been caught in a compromising position. He'd reassured Oam that Samsa wouldn't tell anyone. Since he'd been glaring at her as he said that, Oam had surmised that it was a threat. Luckily, Samsa appeared delighted to find them kissing and had promised she'd keep the secret. Oam could do nothing but trust her. Since Tito did, he felt he could.

He rolled to his side. Both eggs were in the nest with him. Sometimes, he couldn't stop looking at them. He and Tito had agreed that Oam might as well start keeping both eggs together so that Tito wouldn't have to worry. That meant that Oam was spending a lot of time in his room, but he didn't mind. He did that anyway, and this way, he didn't have to worry about Rutger's family. Besides, it wasn't as lonely as it had been before since Tito had insisted that Oam had to have a bodyguard with him at all times.

Oam wasn't sure it was necessary. He was afraid of what Filicia would do when she decided to strike, but she'd never attacked him physically. He felt like having a bodyguard was overkill, but Tito had pointed out that it wasn't just for him. Oam was caring for Tito's egg, and Tito wanted to ensure the egg was safe.

That was why Oam had agreed to have a bodyguard. He didn't want anything to happen to either of the children, and the bodyguard kept an eye on both Tito's egg and his. It meant that Oam was able to relax when he left his room because he knew that if Filicia came up to him, she wouldn't be allowed to hurt him. She could still tell him how much she hated him, but Oam was used to her venom, and he didn't care how she felt about him.

A knock on the door made Oam sit up. He didn't have to be afraid of who was knocking on his door anymore since his guards either stood outside his door or came in with him. "Yes?"

The door opened, and Marlin peeked in. Oam didn't know him well yet, but he liked him and Birch. He still couldn't believe the king's personal bodyguards had been assigned to protect him. He'd been flustered when he'd found out, but both Marlin and Birch had assured him that it was their job and that Killian knew about it and was fine with it. Apparently, he'd decided he didn't need bodyguards in his own palace. Oam wasn't sure that was true, but he hoped it was.

"I have to go," Marlin said. "I got a call from Killian, and he needs me. Birch will be here in ten minutes tops. Is that all right with you?"

"Sure. I'm not going anywhere, and I won't open up to anyone."

Marlin nodded. "Good. I'll see you tomorrow, all right?"

Oam waved at him. Marlin closed the door, and Oam relaxed back in the nest. He hadn't been lying. He had no plans of going anywhere. He was supposed to have lunch with Tito soon, but he had a little time to relax.

A loud crack made him jump. He looked around, then eyed the door and wondered if someone was trying to come in. Maybe someone had been watching and was taking advantage of the fact that Marlon was gone.

Oam realized the sound came from much closer when he heard a second crack. He blinked down at the eggs, then frowned. He leaned even closer, and just then, Tito's egg shuddered and cracked again.

Oam sucked in a breath. He gently touched the surface of the egg, and sure enough, there were small cracks running all over it. How could he have not noticed it? The egg might have been cracking for hours now, and he hadn't realized it.

But he was still in time. Tito had to be there when his child was born, and while the egg was cracking pretty quickly now, it was still whole. The baby inside hadn't yet managed to push any part of the shell off, but they would soon.

Oam jumped out of the nest. He grabbed his egg, almost dropping it when he realized that the surface wasn't smooth anymore. Both eggs were cracking at the same time.

He swore and stuffed his egg into the carrier after putting it on. Then, he grabbed Tito's egg, his phone, and ran out the door.

He didn't stop to think about the fact that he was alone. He just knew he needed to get to Tito, and his feet took him in that direction. He'd been spending so much time in Tito's office that it almost felt like a second home.

But things were never easy in Oam's life. He turned a corner and almost slammed against someone coming the other way. He didn't look to check if they were all right, just continued moving, but they grabbed his arm.

He jerked to a stop and pulled his arm away. He turned, already glaring, then froze when he found Filicia staring at him.

This wasn't what Oam needed right now. She'd pitch a fit if she found out that Oam's egg was cracking. He wouldn't allow her to be there when the baby came out, and she wouldn't like that. She might even try to take his egg, and he was carrying Tito's, so he couldn't defend himself. He wouldn't hurt one baby to save the other, but he also couldn't lose his child.

"Where are you running to?" Filicia asked.

"I have an appointment with Tito. I have to go."

"How did you convince him to be on your side? Did you seduce him like you seduced my son?"

Oam was usually careful of what he did and said when he was with Filicia. Anything could set her off, and he had to keep her happy so she wouldn't take his egg. Right now, though, he was overwhelmed and in a rush, and he snorted before he could think better of it.

Her eyes narrowed. "What are you doing?" she asked again.

"I never seduced your son. I didn't want anything to do with him, and I was forced to have his child. You should be ashamed of yourself." The words poured from Oam's lips. He'd never said them out loud, and he doubted it would change Filicia's behavior, but it felt good to finally be able to tell her what he thought of her. "Your son was a monster, just like you are."

"How dare you?" Filicia's face turned red, and she raised

a hand, probably to slap Oam.

He couldn't stop it since he was still holding Tito's egg, but that was all right. He didn't care if she slapped him. He didn't care if she hated him.

A hand grabbed her wrist, stopping her. She made a strangled sound and turned, no doubt to yell at the person who had stopped her, but she froze when she saw it was Birch.

Oam relaxed. Birch was here, so everything would be all right.

Birch looked from Filicia to Oam. "Everything all right here?"

"I need to see Tito," Oam told him before Filicia could start screeching.

"Let go of me right this instant!" Filicia yelled. "How dare you touch me?"

Oam didn't like the thought of letting Birch deal with Filicia alone, but he didn't have a choice. He had to get to Tito.

Tito was talking to Samsa in her office when he heard loud voices outside in the hallway. Initially, he didn't think much of it, but when the voices rose higher, he frowned and decided to check what was happening. There were plenty of guards to intervene if needed, but he was curious, especially since this was happening just outside the offices.

He opened the door of Samsa's office and froze as he stepped into the hallway.

Why was Filicia yelling at Birch? What was happening?

"I'll have you fired!" Filicia screamed.

For some reason, Birch was holding her wrist. It looked like he'd stopped her from hitting him, and if that was what happened, Tito would make sure she paid for trying to hurt the bodyguard. Birch was more than capable of defending himself from her, but he shouldn't have to.

"You can certainly try," Birch said. He sounded amused.

Filicia's face was so red that Tito thought it couldn't get redder, but he was wrong. It did.

"I have the support of the future king," she spat out. "He won't just have you fired. You'll be kicked out of the clan or, even better, executed for putting your hands on me."

She turned, and Birch let go of her. Tito sucked in a breath when he realized who she turned to. He hadn't recognized Oam standing there because he had his back to Tito, but he did now.

"And you," Filicia continued. Her tone was full of venom. "I will take my grandchild and ensure you can never see them. I might not be able to have you executed, but I can make sure you suffer, and I will."

Tito had enough. It had been one thing for Filicia to have a go at Birch, who could defend himself and had no relationship with her, but she was talking to Oam now. His heart was soft. More than that, no one should have to hear what Filicia had just said.

Tito strode toward them. Oam was watching Filicia, so he didn't see him, but Birch did. Tito nodded at him, silently telling him he could do whatever he felt was necessary to take care of Filicia. Tito would focus on Oam.

"Enough," he snapped when he reached them.

Filicia turned to him with her mouth open as if she was going to threaten him, too. Birch grabbed her arm and pulled her back, stopping her before she could do anything stupid. Tito took the opportunity to pull Oam away. Oam had his egg in the carrier and was holding Tito's, so Tito couldn't take his hand, but that didn't matter. Oam allowed him to guide him toward his office.

"What's going on?" Tito asked.

"She cornered me. I know I'm not supposed to go anywhere without a bodyguard, but your egg started cracking, and I couldn't wait for Birch to arrive."

Tito swore. "Why didn't you call me? I would have come to you."

"I don't know. I didn't think about it, but you could have been in a meeting. I just knew I had to get to your office."

Tito ushered Oam inside. Samsa was hovering by the door, looking worried. She stood up straighter when Tito looked at her.

"Keep everyone away except for Killian. The egg is cracking."

Samsa's eyes widened, and she nodded. "Of course."

"Also, please contact Alcen."

"Right away. I'll also organize a snack. You go into your office and lock the door."

She didn't have to say it twice. She had the key, as did Killian, so only the people who Tito wanted there would be able to enter.

Oam relaxed as soon as they stepped into Tito's office. Tito quickly locked the door, then turned. He wasn't sure he was ready to meet his child, but he didn't have a choice. The baby was coming, whether he liked it or not.

Oam strode toward the couches. The small nest Tito had put together was still there, and Oam was incredibly gentle as he settled Tito's egg into it. He hesitated, then took his own egg out of the carrier and put it next to Tito's. "I noticed mine had cracked, too."

Tito gaped. "They're hatching together?"

"Looks like it. Maybe it's normal? One of them could have realized the other was hatching and decided to do the same. I don't know much about eggs and children. I should have looked into it."

Tito stepped forward and wrapped an arm around Oam's waist. "We both should have. It's too late now. Besides, what does it change? Both eggs were always going to hatch."

Oam leaned against Tito's side. The two of them turned their attention to the eggs, and now that they were under the light streaming in from the window, Tito could see the cracks on both surfaces.

He yelped when his egg shuddered and a piece of the shell fell off the top. He had to resist the urge to help the baby come out. Alcen had warned him and Oam that they'd both feel they needed to do something, but the babies could do this on their own. If it took too long, they could step in, but for now, it was safer to allow the babies to do this at their own pace.

That didn't mean Tito couldn't peek inside.

He sat on one side of the nest, eager to be closer to the babies. Oam did the same on the other side, and they both leaned over the eggs. Their gazes caught as they moved, and Tito smiled.

He'd thought he would have to do this on his own, but Oam was by his side. They'd live this moment together, which made Tito feel better. Neither of them knew what they were doing with the eggs, but they would find out together.

Oam watched in awe as the eggs shuddered and cracked. He wasn't worried, but he was eager for Alcen to get there. The healer had kept an eye on both the eggs. He'd assured both Oam and Tito that everything was going smoothly, but Oam would feel better once he was there.

In theory, he knew what to do with a newborn dragon. He and Tito had to wait for the babies to get out of their eggs on their own. If it took too long, Alcen would intervene, but for now, the babies were on their own.

Oam wasn't sure he liked that. He wanted to help, especially once the first bits of shells started falling. It was hard to keep his hands to himself, and he stuck them under his thighs.

Tito snickered. "It's hard, isn't it?"

"I just want to help. They're so little and are already fighting for their lives."

Tito reached for Oam's knee and squeezed it. "They'll be fine. We're here to help if they need it, and Alcen will arrive soon. He'll know what to do better than we do."

Oam didn't doubt that since neither he nor Tito had any idea what they were doing.

The only thing they could do was watch as the eggs continued cracking. More and more pieces fell, and Oam leaned so close that he almost brushed what remained of the shell of his egg with his nose.

A tiny eye blinked open and stared back at him.

Oam jerked back, surprised, only to laugh and lean forward again. It took him a moment to make sense of his baby's position. As the baby grew inside the egg, there had been less and less space available for them, and they'd curled up. They didn't have enough space to stretch out, but they would soon. In the meantime, Oam could see that his baby's head was firmly pressed against their stomach. Their tail was wrapped around most of their body, making them a little ball of baby dragon. It was adorable.

"What color is yours?" Tito asked.

"The same pale blue as I am."

The baby looked like the egg it had been in. Oam was glad because it meant there would be no reminders of Rutger when he looked at his child. If anything, the specks of dark pink on his baby's skin reminded him of Tito. Tito wasn't the baby's second father, but he could have been considering the baby's colors.

Tito gasped, and Oam looked over to see that his child was halfway out of the egg. The baby stretched and raised their head toward the ceiling, yawning.

It was adorable.

The baby was a similar color to Tito, dark magenta, but

they tended a bit more toward purple. It was almost like there was blue in there, too, and even though the four of them weren't a family, it would be so easy to believe they were related. Maybe it was a sign. Even if it wasn't, Oam liked to think it was. They looked like they belonged together, and he hoped Tito felt they did.

Because he did.

Tito's child stumbled as they tried to get to their feet and fell against Oam's egg. Oam gasped and attempted to keep it upright, but he wasn't fast enough, and it fell sideways. Thankfully, the egg was still in the nest, so it didn't shatter. His baby blinked, then poked their head out of the egg.

That was when they saw Tito's baby.

Oam hadn't known baby dragons could move so quickly. One moment, his baby was still inside the egg, and the next, they were kicking at what remained of the shell and pushing it away so they could rush toward Tito's child. Thankfully, they didn't have to go far because their legs were wobbly. They fell face-first into the nest. Since Oam and Tito could help now, Oam did just that. He gently put his child back on their feet, getting their attention.

For a moment, the baby looked torn between wanting to go to Oam and wanting to go to Tito's child. There was nothing Oam wanted more than to pick up his child and hug them, but this felt like an important moment. Over the past few weeks, the eggs had spent most of their time together. The children inside hadn't been born then, but Oam thought it was obvious they'd been aware of each other. He didn't think they would have hatched at the same time if they hadn't been.

He ran his fingertips down his baby's back. "You're finally here," he murmured.

The baby chirped and bumped their face against Oam's fingers. Oam laughed, delighted, before watching as his child stumbled toward Tito's baby. The two babies fell against each other as someone knocked on the door.

Tito got to his feet. He didn't hesitate to leave the babies with Oam, which touched Oam. It had been one thing to have Oam watch the eggs, but the babies? That was a completely different thing.

Tito ushered Alcen inside. The healer made a beeline for the nest, beaming when he saw the hatching had gone perfectly.

"They didn't need my help," he said as he put down his bag and crouched next to the couch.

"They did all of it on their own. I think they spurred each other on," Tito explained. He sat back down on the couch, a soft smile playing on his lips. "They haven't really been interested in Oam and me."

Alcen nodded. "I'm not surprised. The two of them sensed each other while they were in their eggs and were eager to meet each other."

"Is it always like that?" Oam asked.

"Most of the time when two eggs are raised together," Alcen confirmed. "It often happened when we kept the eggs together before. It doesn't mean the babies will be best friends, but there's a good chance they will be as long as you don't separate them."

Oam glanced at Tito, who was already shaking his head.

"We're not going to separate them," Tito said. "We're a family."

Oam felt both the need to laugh and cry. They *were* a family, and it felt good to hear Tito confirm that. Oam had felt that way for a while, but he was always a bit hesitant. He still didn't understand what Tito saw in him, but he'd realized that it didn't matter.

Alcen offered one of his hands for the babies to sniff. Tito's child was cautious, but Oam's rushed forward, falling on their face. Oam laughed and quickly put them back on their feet, which caused them to chirp again.

Alcen spoke to the babies in a soft voice. He didn't say much, just told them how beautiful they were and that he was so happy to meet them, but it warmed Oam's heart. No matter what happened in the future, the babies would be protected by the clan. The four of them were a family, but the clan was their family, too.

"I don't have to ask to know which baby belongs to whom," Alcen said as he gently picked up Oam's child.

Oam held his breath and watched as Alcen checked the baby. He didn't know what Alcen was looking for, but from Alcen's expression, he found it, which was a relief.

"This little lady is perfect," Alcen said.

Oam beamed. "A girl?"

"Unless she decides otherwise, yes," Alcen confirmed. "Have you thought of a name?"

Oam and Tito had talked about names for a while. It hadn't been easy to choose one, and while Tito had picked two names depending on what sex the baby would be, Oam had chosen a more unisex one. "Daron."

Alcen handed Daron to Oam before turning his attention to Tito's baby. He seemed satisfied as he handled them, so Oam was reassured that both babies were all right. "A boy," Alcen said as he handed over the baby to Tito, who cradled him in his arms.

"Sandor," Tito said with a nod.

"Well, both Sandor and Daron are perfect and healthy. The two of you have nothing to worry about. While you'll have to keep an eye on them for the next few days especially, I don't think there will be any complications."

Oam cradled Daron against his chest. It felt odd after holding an egg for so long. Daron wasn't still and quiet like the egg had been. She wriggled against Oam as if wanting to be put down, but Oam wasn't ready to do that yet.

He and Tito looked at each other. Their lives had just massively changed, but neither of them would want it any other way.

CHAPTER TEN

Tito had the hardest time focusing on work. He'd thought things were bad when Killian and the others had been with the Ogorth clan right before the final fight, but this was even worse.

He wasn't worried about Sandor. The baby was with Oam, so Tito knew he was safe and healthy. If anything happened, Oam would call him right away.

It was just hard to be away from the baby. Tito had taken a few days off right after the hatching, mostly because Killian had threatened to fire him if he didn't. He felt he couldn't step away from his job for too long, so two days had been a compromise. As much as Tito wanted to stay with Sandor for weeks, he couldn't afford to do so.

The baby was with someone Tito trusted with his life, but knowing that Sandor was safe didn't help Tito focus. It felt like every second of every day, he wondered what Sandor was up to. Thankfully, there was an easy way for him to find out.

He grabbed his phone from the desk and quickly dialed Oam's number. He'd called Oam so often lately that it was the first number to come up on his phone. It made him smile, and not just because of the babies.

He and Oam were together. They hadn't talked about it yet, but they would. They just needed things to settle down first, and Tito hoped they would soon. It wasn't only the babies, although they were a big part of why he and Oam hadn't had the opportunity to talk yet. They took a lot of energy and attention, which was natural but left Tito feeling a bit out of his depth. He wasn't used to focusing so much on only one person.

"They're fine," Oam said when he answered. "They just had a snack, and they're going to have a nap soon."

Tito chuckled. "You know me so well."

"I do. I don't want you to worry about anything. I'm not planning on leaving my room today, so no one is going to intercept me, and if they try coming to me, Marlin is right outside the door. I'm fine. We all are."

Tito relaxed in his chair. "I couldn't do this without you."

"Good thing you don't have to."

It *was* a good thing. Tito wasn't sure what he would do if Oam wasn't available to keep Sandor, but even more than that, he didn't *want* Oam not to be available. He wanted them to do this together, as a family.

Sometimes Tito wondered if it was the right thing to do. His life was chaotic, and being Killian's best friend meant there was always a spotlight on him. In turn, it meant it would be on Oam if they continued their relationship.

Tito was pretty sure it was too late to be cautious. He and Oam were in this together, whatever happened. It meant that Tito would have to be especially cautious.

A knock on his door made him look up. It was closed, but Samsa wouldn't have allowed anyone to knock if it weren't necessary, so Tito knew he had to go. "Someone's here," he told Oam.

"I'll see you tonight. Don't worry about me or the babies. I have everything in hand."

"I'm not worried. I just miss you."

Oam sucked in a breath. "We miss you, too."

Tito didn't want to make whoever was at his door wait, so he quickly hung up even though there was nothing he wanted less. "Come in," he called out.

The door opened, and Tito knew he wouldn't like whatever was about to be said. "I consider you a friend, Birch, but lately, you haven't brought me good news," he said as the bodyguard walked in.

Birch grimaced. "And I don't have any good news now, either."

"Is it Killian?"

"For once, no. It's Filicia. Nothing happened, but I think we need to talk about her and what she's probably planning."

He was right. It was even more important to talk about her now that Oam's egg had hatched. She'd been insistent that she wanted the baby before, but now that there was an actual baby, she wouldn't stop unless forced to. Tito didn't know her well, but he knew the kind of person she was and had looked into her.

Birch sat in one of the chairs in front of Tito's desk and leaned forward, placing his elbows on his knees. "I'm worried about what she said about having the ear of the future king."

Tito remembered that. He should have worried about it sooner, but it had been easy to ignore with everything that happened that day. "What do you think she meant?"

"Your guess is as good as mine, but we both know that some of Killian's siblings are assholes. I can think of at least a few of them who wouldn't think anything of killing Killian to get the throne."

Tito tapped his fingertips on top of his desk. "And you think Filicia is allied with one of them."

"I think considering what she said, that makes sense."

"Do we know who?"

"Not yet. I've been looking into it, but I don't want her to realize we're onto her. It doesn't really matter, anyway. Whoever she's allied with, if they want Killian's throne, they're dangerous. I've looked a bit into her, and she has quite a bit of influence and power. Her son, Daron's second father, was one of Eldar's personal bodyguards. From what I learned, the two of them were quite close, and Rutger was as cruel as the king."

"Oam said something about Rutger asking to be the person Oam would have a child with," Tito confirmed. "The king gave him what he wanted, so I'm not surprised they were close. That means that Rutger's family can be a problem, though."

"Just give the order, and I'll make sure they can't bother you and Killian."

Tito rolled his eyes. "We're not there yet. I want to keep an eye on them, but more importantly, I need to keep my children safe. I need to talk to Killian about this. He has to know that at least one of his brothers is aiming for the throne."

"I'm sure he already knows."

"He does. He was able to ignore it before, but now that the war is over, we have to deal with it."

And with a bunch of other problems. Every time Tito thought about how much work he had, his head started pounding. He'd hoped that with the war over, he'd finally be able to relax and that he might have time to be with his child and his family, but clearly, that wouldn't happen. If he wanted Oam and the babies to be safe, he needed to keep the clan safe, and that meant making sure that anyone who tried to reach the throne failed.

Killian was King Eldar's only official heir. He was the king's only child with the queen, which meant his place was on the throne. More importantly, he was the only one of the king's children who would make a good king.

That meant Tito needed to do whatever was in his power to keep Killian on the throne. Apparently, doing so would kill two birds with one stone. If it got rid of Filicia for Oam, too, then Tito would do so happily.

He just had to find out what they were planning first.

Oam could tell something was wrong as soon as he opened the door and saw Tito's expression. He almost asked what was going on, but it probably had to do with Tito's job, and Oam didn't want Tito to feel like he was intruding on something that wasn't his business.

"They're both asleep," he whispered as he let Tito in.

Tito visibly relaxed. "I'm sorry, I'm late," he whispered back.

"Don't be. I know how important your job is, and it's not a problem. Are you going to take him back now? Or would you rather leave him be while he's sleeping?" Oam wanted Tito and the baby to stay, but he didn't dare ask.

Maybe he should. After all, he and Tito were together, or at least, Oam thought so. They hadn't had the time to talk about what had happened in Tito's office. Tito had been overwhelmed with work, and then with the baby. He had much better things to focus on than Oam, but Oam still wanted to be the center of his attention. It was selfish, but sometimes, he wondered if being a little selfish was that bad for him.

He didn't think so.

"How high are the chances I'll wake him if I try taking him home?" Tito asked as he moved toward the small nest they'd set up in the corner.

"Well, they just fell asleep."

Tito raised the corner of the nest covering. The nest was well insulated so the babies wouldn't get cold, and it was built so that light and noise wouldn't bother them. With so many people living in the palace, keeping young children in these nests was necessary.

Oam moved next to Tito and looked in the nest. The babies were adorable. Daron and Sandor were curled around each other, looking like they belonged. Oam liked to think they did. He and Tito were still finding their way together, but since Oam was watching both children while Tito worked, they were growing up together. They'd hatched simultaneously, and it had felt like the beginning of something.

Tito's shoulders slumped. "As long as I'm not bothering you, we'll stay a while longer."

"You could never bother me."

Once Tito had replaced the covering, Oam guided him toward his nest. Maybe the couch would have been better, but Tito was physically exhausted, so he might want to take a nap.

Sometimes, Oam felt it was ridiculous that after he'd spent the entire day watching Sandor, Tito took him home. They were together, so why shouldn't they share the same living spaces? Why shouldn't the babies stay together?

Tito and Oam hadn't talked about that yet, either. They needed to have a long conversation, but Oam wasn't sure when they could have it. Tito worked every day, and Oam was busy with the babies. Sometimes, it felt like he and Tito barely had the time to see each other. They were both exhausted and working around the babies and Killian's schedules.

Oam sighed. He was getting ahead of himself. He and Tito had made out a few times, but that could be all there was to it on Tito's side. Maybe he just liked Oam well enough to kiss him but didn't want anything more with him, or maybe he did but didn't have the time and energy to deal with it.

Tito flopped into Oam's nest and stretched out. He looked at home there, but Oam told himself not to obsess over that. If things between them were meant to be, they'd happen. It might take some time, but it would.

He sat down next to Tito and took his hand. Tito didn't say anything, so Oam started massaging it. He could feel Tito's entire body was tense, and he wasn't sure how to help.

"I talked to Birch earlier," Tito said.

Oam wasn't sure why Tito was telling him that. "You talk to him every day, don't you?"

"I do. Usually, it's about Killian, but it was about you this time."

Oam swallowed. "Why? Did something happen?"

The news that the babies had hatched had run through the clan like wildfire. Everyone knew it by now, and while Oam tried to stay in his room as much as possible, every time he stepped out, someone congratulated him. He never left the room alone after what had happened with Rutger's mother, but knowing her, she was plotting something. She wanted Oam's daughter and would do anything to get her.

"No, but we both agree that something will eventually. I know you don't want to talk about it, but can you tell me more about Daron's biological father?"

Oam had known this would happen. He was pretty sure Tito knew how Daron had been conceived, but he might need more details to deal with Filicia.

Oam closed his eyes and squeezed Tito's hand. "There's nothing much to say. I went to one of the mandatory visits to the infirmary, and the healer noticed I was about to be fertile. She let the king know. I was supposed to be able to choose who I wanted to have a child with, but instead, Rutger told me he would be the other father of my child. I tried to argue, but no one would listen to me."

Oam's mouth was dry. He could too easily remember what had happened that day. They'd been in the infirmary. He wouldn't have been able to live in this room if this was where his daughter had been conceived.

"I didn't want to do it, but the alternative was to have the healer knock me out, and I couldn't stand that thought. I just lay there and let Rutger do what he was there for. He tried to have a relationship with me after it was done, as if we were in love or something, but I wanted nothing to do with him.

That's when he and his family started harassing me. Once they realized I was pregnant, they were sure they would get to raise the baby, probably because Rutger was one of the king's bodyguards. I knew they were right, and I hated it."

"But then Killian became king."

"Actually, Rutger died. It happened when the Ogorth clan members escaped. He was killed in the attack, and his mother became even more obsessed with my child. She's ready to do anything to raise my daughter, but I can't allow that to happen. I'm a good father, Tito."

Tito sat up and gathered Oam into his arms. "I know you are. I wouldn't leave my son with you if I didn't believe you could raise him."

Oam snuggled against Tito. "I never want to think about Rutger again, and I'm glad he's dead. If his family was different, I might have allowed them to have a relationship with Daron, but not like this. Not when Filicia is trying to take my daughter away from me entirely. She shouldn't be allowed to raise children."

Tito kissed Oam's forehead. "I won't let anything happen to you or your daughter. I promise."

Oam couldn't remember the last time he'd felt so safe. Being in Tito's arms made him feel like nothing bad would happen to him, even though he had difficulty believing that. He wanted to believe nothing bad would ever happen to him and his daughter. He wanted to believe that from now on, he could be happy.

"I know," he whispered.

He tilted his head up to look at Tito. Tito was staring at him in a way that made Oam feel all fluttery inside. Oam leaned up and kissed him.

He didn't expect much, but as soon as their lips touched, he knew this kiss was different. Tito was still holding him, but the position wasn't comfortable for them to kiss, so Oam wasn't surprised when Tito moved him. He wasn't sure how he ended up on his back, but he wasn't about to protest when Tito knelt between his legs and looked at him with lust in his gaze.

Oam was happy to follow Tito's lead. He didn't mind having Tito tell him what to do. He trusted him with his life and with his daughter's.

Tito leaned forward and stuck his tongue out. Oam's body flushed, and his cock peeked from its pouch. Oam had to resist the urge to hide his face. He'd never felt what he felt for Tito for anyone else, and this encounter felt completely different from every other time he'd had sex, especially the last time.

It was incredibly cheesy, but this wasn't having sex. It was making love, at least on Oam's side.

Tito flicked his tongue over the tip of Oam's cock. Oam shuddered and leaned back, opening his body up to Tito. Tito's tongue slithered around Oam's cock, rubbing against it as Tito leaned closer, then sucked the head.

Oam could only lie there and take whatever Tito threw at him. Tito lavished Oam's cock for a while, driving him nuts but not enough to make him come. That didn't change when Tito moved down to tease the edge of Oam's pouch with his tongue. He ran the tip up and down the edges, then stuck it inside to lick at the root of Oam's cock.

Oam's tail ran up and down Tito's back. He didn't know what to do with it, and he wasn't sure he had enough control to use it to make Tito feel as good as Tito was making him feel, but he could try.

He slid it around Tito's waist and wrapped it around Tito's cock. Tito looked up, and their gazes crossed. There was so much heat in the way Tito looked at Oam that it made Oam want to beg him to take him. He almost did, but Tito wasn't done with him.

Oam hoped he never would be.

Tito's tail slithered between Oam's thighs. Oam sucked in a breath when he felt the tip slip into his pouch. It stroked around the base of his cock, but not for long. When it retreated, Oam felt it slide down his body.

To his hole.

It felt like Tito was everywhere at once. He was lavishing Oam's cock, teasing Oam's pouch with his fingers, and pushing inside of him with his tail. Oam was surrounded by Tito, and he loved it.

He loved Tito.

He opened his mouth to scream it, but the only thing that came out was a croak. Maybe it was for the best. It didn't feel like telling Tito he loved him in this situation would be the best way to do it. Oam wanted Tito closer, though, and he scrambled to grab Tito's shoulders.

Tito let go of Oam's cock with a pop and pressed his cheek against Oam's inner thigh. It was easier to think without Tito's mouth on him, but not that easy because Tito was still touching Oam. He had two fingers inside Oam's pouch and was fucking him with his tail.

"What do you want?" Tito asked.

Oam glared at him, grabbed him under the armpits, and tried to pull him up. Tito was heavier than he looked, and he didn't move, so Oam glared at him harder.

Tito grinned and slid his fingers out of Oam's pouch. His tail retreated from Oam's ass, only to slide around his thigh and push inside of him again from under him. Like this, Tito would have enough space to plunge into Oam's pouch while he still was inside Oam's ass.

The thought was almost enough to make Oam come.

He stared as Tito leaned over him and captured his lips. They kissed while Tito settled on top of Oam, and Oam opened his legs wider. He'd never wanted anyone the way he wanted Tito, and he was reminded of why when Tito stopped before pushing inside of him.

"Everything all right?" he asked in a whisper.

Oam knew why he was asking and what he was thinking about. He hated that Tito felt he needed to do it, but at the same time, he was grateful because it meant Tito truly cared about him.

He was nothing like Rutger, and what they were doing was nothing like what Rutger had done to Oam.

Oam nodded and pulled Tito closer again. He felt Tito's cock slide inside his pouch, rubbing against his, and bit Tito's lower lip so he wouldn't scream. The palace's walls were thick, but not that thick. He didn't want his neighbors to wonder what was happening.

It wouldn't last much longer, anyway. With Tito fucking both Oam's pouch and his ass, the sensations were too much. Oam's body felt like he was about to explode, and he couldn't wait. He grabbed Tito's ass, digging his fingers into the meaty flesh before dragging his fingertips up to the base of Tito's tail. When he reached it, he stroked around it, then down between Tito's ass cheeks.

Tito growled and fucked Oam harder. Their bodies made a squelching sound because of how wet Oam was. He could feel his slickness slide down from his pouch to his ass, easing the way for Tito's cock.

The friction inside Oam's pouch was maddening, but he needed more. He slipped his tail between their bodies and wrapped it around his cock.

That was what he needed. He stroked himself at the same rhythm Tito was fucking him and saw stars. His entire body contracted, and he dimly heard Tito groan. He was lost to anything that wasn't his pleasure. He came harder than he could ever remember coming.

He was barely coming down from his pleasure when Tito

came, too. Thankfully, Oam wasn't fertile and wouldn't be for several years, so he didn't have to worry about getting pregnant. Neither of them could deal with another child right now.

But maybe, one day.

Oam dropped his arms and legs to the nest. He was breathing hard, and his entire body felt heavy. He was pretty sure he would fall asleep in seconds if he allowed himself to, but first, he had to deal with Tito.

Tito flopped next to him, but he didn't go far. He hooked an arm and a leg around Oam, almost as if he was afraid Oam would try to escape. Oam wasn't going anywhere since this was his room, but he wanted to know what to expect.

"Stay the night?" he asked.

Tito kissed him. "You don't have to ask. There's nowhere I'd rather be, my love."

The reassurance was enough for Oam to allow himself to drift off to sleep. He'd have to wake up soon enough when the babies would need him, but for now, he could let Tito hold him and tell himself that nothing but their small family mattered.

CHAPTER ELEVEN

For all that Tito's life was complicated, he couldn't be happier. That had everything to do with Oam and the babies and nothing to do with his job and the people he had to deal with. If he could, he'd take a yearlong vacation and ignore all of the clan's problems, but unfortunately, doing so would be dangerous, and that wasn't something Tito was willing to allow.

That meant he was working his ass off.

He'd talked to Killian about whichever of his siblings had targeted the throne, and while Killian agreed it was worrying, he'd also pointed out that it wasn't anything new. He had a lot of faith in his power and ability to stay on the throne. Tito hoped he was right. They couldn't allow anyone else to get the throne and the clan. They were still recovering from everything Killian's father had done and from the war, and it would take almost nothing to plunge the clan into a desperate situation.

Knowing all of that didn't change how happy Tito was. He whistled as he quickly walked down the hallway, headed toward his office. He'd wanted to stay with Oam and the babies today, but since he couldn't, he'd try to get back to them as soon as possible.

That plan went right out the window when he walked into Samsa's office and found Filicia there.

The two dragons were facing each other. Samsa had her arms crossed over her chest as she glared at Filicia, who looked ready to strangle her. Tito would have paid to watch that fight, but he liked Samsa, and he didn't want her to have to resort to violence, even though she looked ready to do just that.

"What's going on here?" he asked, putting all of his authority into his voice.

Filicia jumped, but Samsa didn't. She was still glaring. "She said she wanted to talk to Killian, and when I told her he was unavailable today, she started yelling at me."

"I *demand* to see the king," Filicia said.

She raised her chin and looked down at Tito. Well, she would have looked down at him if she'd been taller, but unfortunately for her, he towered over her. She still did her best to look at him as if he was nothing more than a fly on the wall, but he didn't care. He was used to dealing with these kinds of people. He had been since he was a child. Some people hadn't taken him being Killian's best friend well because he came from a modest family, and he hadn't cared any more then than he did now.

"I can check Killian's schedule for you, but I can already tell you that Samsa is right. The king doesn't have time to see you today," he said.

"It is my right to talk to him."

"I can make you an appointment."

"I don't trust you. You're involved in this, so I have to talk directly to the king."

Tito was tempted to tell her to fuck off. Unfortunately — or fortunately, because Tito had enough of dealing with Filicia — Killian's office door opened.

Usually that door was locked, but clearly, Killian had heard the commotion and wanted to investigate. He could have done so through Tito's office, and Tito wasn't sure why he hadn't, but he scowled at him so his friend knew he was unhappy with what he was doing.

"What's going on?" Killian asked. He looked around the

room, then at Tito.

Filicia bowed. She didn't even try to look like she respected Killian. Her bow should have been deeper, and she shouldn't be staring at the king the way she was now.

Tito resisted the urge to snap at her. He didn't really care what Filicia thought of him or Killian. As long as she followed Killian's authority, the way she behaved didn't matter.

Or maybe it did. Maybe Killian should punish her for being so disrespectful. That way, she'd be out of Tito and Oam's hair, and they could finally focus on their happiness. Either way, something would have to be done about her soon.

"Your Majesty," she said. "I need to talk to you about my grandchild."

Killian frowned. "I'm sorry, but I don't know who you are or who your grandchild is."

Tito grinned. From the expression on Filicia's face, she didn't like that, which meant he loved it. He didn't want her to have the upper hand, so he quickly answered. "Her granddaughter is Oam's daughter."

"Oam is incapable of raising a child. He's weak, and after what he did to my son, you can't allow him to raise my granddaughter."

Killian frowned. "Why do you think he's incapable of raising a child? I've talked to him several times, and he's delightful."

Tito was used to Filicia looking like she wanted to murder someone when she talked to him, and today wasn't any different.

He loved it.

"That dragon seduced my son," she spat out. "After my son died, he refused to allow me access to the egg, and now, he won't let me meet my granddaughter."

"Maybe that's because you want to take her from him," Killian pointed out.

"He shouldn't be allowed to raise her. My family and I are better suited to raising a child, and we'll give her anything she might want. He doesn't have that kind of resources available."

"Again, I don't see why it means he can't raise his daughter. I'm sorry, but he's her father, which is why the egg was given to him. Unless I have serious reasons to believe he isn't a good father, there's nothing I can or want to do about this situation. If that's all, I have work to do."

"I knew you'd say that. Oam seduced your assistant, too, and I'm sure he did it to get to you. He knew what he was doing, but you can't see it. You're on his side because of Tito."

That was the wrong thing to say. Killian straightened his back and squared his shoulders, and when he stared down Filicia, he was every bit the king Tito knew him to be. Tito didn't usually see him like this, and he didn't like how cold Killian was right now, but it was what was needed in this situation.

"I have seen Oam with his daughter," Killian said. "He's a good father, so much so that my best friend asked him to raise his son, too. Unless you have concrete proof that Oam shouldn't be raising his daughter, this conversation is over."

Filicia looked like a stubborn child who'd been sent in timeout. "You'll regret this. If you don't give me my granddaughter, I'll make sure your brother wins the throne."

That gave Killian pause, but not for long. He glared at Filicia as if *she* was the fly on the wall. "I don't know which one of my brothers you've decided to ally yourself with, and I honestly don't care. Whoever it is, it won't end well for either of you. You might still have a chance to have a relationship with your granddaughter, but I doubt Oam will ever want you near her, and I don't blame him. Maybe you should think about your behavior instead of plotting how you can ruin Oam's life." He looked at Tito. "Can you come to my office?"

Tito was quick to follow him. "Of course, your Majesty," he said as he glared at Filicia.

Something was going to have to be done about her. Tito had hoped they could just ignore her, but she might be more dangerous than they expected, and they couldn't afford to ignore an enemy.

No matter how much they wanted to.

Oam wasn't surprised that Tito called him a few times that day. He did so every day, mostly to check on them. Usually, Oam could reassure him easily, but today had been different.

That was why Oam expected something to have happened. He hadn't asked Tito, even though he wanted to know. He suspected he'd find out soon enough, anyway. If something had happened, Tito would want Oam to be able to defend himself, which meant that he needed to know what was going on.

Tito walked in right away when Oam opened the door after he knocked. Oam peeked into the hallway, smiled at Birch, then closed the door.

Instead of making a beeline for the sitting area where the babies were climbing on and off the couch, Tito grabbed Oam and pulled him into his arms. Oam hugged him and stroked his back, unsure what to do or say to make him feel better. "What happened?"

Tito's shoulders slumped. "I wish we didn't have to talk about this."

"We do."

Tito stepped away, taking Oam's hand and pulling him toward the couch. Sandor squeaked when he saw his father and rushed to him, and Tito took a moment to say hello. It didn't last long. Daron and Sandor had so much fun together that they seldom paid a lot of attention to the rest of the world, including their fathers. Alcen had reassured Tito and Oam that it was normal. The babies knew who their fathers were and that with them, they were safe, and that was all that mattered.

Tito flopped back against the couch and stared at the ceiling for a moment. Oam sat next to him, giving him the time he needed to put his thoughts into order. He'd already learned that pushing Tito wouldn't help. He needed time to process things, and that was fine with Oam. It wasn't like he was looking forward to being told what was wrong. In fact, he wished he never had to find out, but unfortunately, he needed to know, if he wanted to keep his daughter safe.

Tito finally straightened and looked at Oam. "Filicia made a scene in the office today."

Oam winced. He could imagine all too well what had happened, and it wasn't pleasant. It had to have been worse to live through it. "I'm sorry."

Tito shook his head. "There's nothing for you to be sorry about. It wasn't your fault."

"Maybe not, but whatever she did, she did it because of me and because she wants Daron. I wish I could find a way to get her to stop."

"Birch and I are looking into it, but you know her. She's quite influential and has the ear of many of the dragons who work with Killian. We have to be cautious, and while Killian won't hesitate to get rid of her if she as much as tries anything with you or him, for now, she hasn't."

"What did she want?"

Oam didn't think he'd ever hated anyone more. Well, he'd hated Rutger, but the dragon was dead. As much as Oam hated him, he was safe from him.

But not from Filicia.

"The baby, like before. She wanted to talk to Killian, and even though Samsa and I told her he wasn't available today, she insisted. She started yelling, and he heard her, so he walked in to see what was happening. That's when she threatened him."

Oam sucked in a breath. "She threatened him?"

"She told him that one of his brothers was going to take over the throne and that she supported that brother. She didn't say his name, but we're looking into that, too. It's clear that she won't stop for anything to get Daron, though, and I'm worried."

Oam was, too. He'd been staying in his room, safe behind a door and a bodyguard, but could he do that forever? His daughter didn't deserve to be stuck in one room for the rest of her childhood, and neither did Sandor. Eventually, Tito would realize that, and he'd take Sandor away. It would be the right thing to do, but Oam didn't want that to happen.

"What do we do next?" he asked, even though he didn't expect Tito to have a solution.

"I'd like for you to move in with me."

Oam blinked. "What?"

Tito slid closer to Oam and took his hand. "I've been thinking about it. Filicia isn't the only reason I want you and Daron to move in with me. I'm tired of leaving the two of you behind every evening, and so is Sandor. Every night, when we go home, he starts crying because he wants his sister. They might not be related by blood, but they feel like siblings, and I believe that's what makes them family. I don't want to leave you anymore. Moving in with me will keep you safe, but even more importantly, it'll make all of us happier."

Oam hadn't expected that, but maybe he should have. After all, he and Tito were serious about each other. Tito trusted Oam with his son, who was the most precious thing he had. He hadn't told Oam he loved him, but Oam could see that he did every day. There was no one more worried about Oam's safety than Tito, not even Oam's family. They kept inviting him to leave his room, brushing his worries off when he mentioned Filicia. They didn't fully understand what she was capable of, but that was fine with Oam. He didn't want them to because they'd be afraid if they did.

But Tito knew everything. He knew what he was getting himself into, yet he'd still asked Oam to move in with him.

Oam wanted to say yes. He wanted to know that he was safe and that his children wouldn't be taken from him and to live with Tito. They were already a family, and it was ridiculous that they were separated.

He hoped he wasn't making a mistake. He didn't think he was, but only the future would tell, and if he wanted to find out, he'd have to say yes.

He leaned forward and kissed Tito's cheek. "Of course we'll move in with you."

Tito relaxed and pulled Oam into his arms. "Thank the sky. I wasn't going to push if you said no, but I don't think I can continue leaving you behind at night and wondering if you're safe."

"You won't have to anymore. Daron and I are going home with you and Sandor tonight."

Tito beamed. "Yeah, you are."

Something brushed against Oam's foot, and he looked down to see Sandor trying to climb up his leg. He leaned down and grabbed the baby dragon, hauling him into his arms. Sandor made a trilling sound and settled into Oam's lap, quickly followed by Daron.

These two were never far from each other, and they'd grow up together. They'd truly be a family.

No matter how scared Oam was of Filicia and what she was planning, it was easy to ignore all of it tonight. She'd still be a problem tomorrow. Oam wouldn't face her alone. He had Tito, and with him came Killian. Oam had the support of the king.

Hopefully, that would be enough for Filicia to leave him alone.

CHAPTER TWELVE

Tito walked into Killian's office for the meeting, but his mind wasn't on the Ogorth clan. He'd gone over the accounts again, and the situation was dire. They needed the Saganto clan money to come in sooner rather than later.

They had enough money to survive. The clan wouldn't be needing anything just yet, but they might have to pause the renovations, and, more importantly, Tito was afraid that Filicia and Killian's brother would take advantage of the problems. Filicia and her family were wealthy. It would be easy to offer her family's wealth and use it to bolster whichever of Killian's brothers threatened the throne. If they found out how much money trouble the clan and Killian were in, they could use that to take the throne, which was something Tito wouldn't even consider.

Today, Killian would be talking to the Ogorth clan queen and her human ambassador. Tito hoped they'd have good news about the Saganto clan money. He told himself not to have too much hope in case it didn't happen, but he wasn't sure what they'd do if they got bad news.

Killian looked up from his phone, and from his guilty expression, Tito knew he wasn't working. He rolled his eyes as Killian quickly put the phone down.

"I'm not your mother. I'm not going to scold you because you're playing around instead of working."

Killian grinned. "I'm just waiting until the meeting starts. Will you be sitting next to me?"

Tito eyed the desk. Killian was firmly seated behind it, as

124

he should be. Sometimes it was odd to see him there and remember he truly was the king. They'd planned for it for a long time, but to Tito, Killian was just his best friend.

Not anymore. To everyone else, he was King Killian. Tito wasn't sure he'd ever be able to see him that way, but he couldn't deny his friend was doing a good job—as good as he could considering the mess his father had left behind.

Killian's computer beeped, and he turned his attention to it. Tito quickly settled into one of the chairs on the other side of the desk. He didn't need to be in on the meeting.

Killian rolled his eyes and waved at him to move around the desk as he greeted the Ogorth clan queen. "Ita, it's a pleasure to see you. Gideon, hi."

"We shouldn't let so much time pass between two meetings," Ita said. "How are you, Killian? Why are you waving?"

"I'm trying to convince Tito to come sit next to me so you can see him." Killian looked at Tito. "They both know you. They know you're my assistant and best friend. They don't care that you're sitting in on this meeting."

"Congratulations on your son, Tito," Ita said.

As much as Tito wanted to stay behind the scenes, Queen Ita had addressed him directly, and it wouldn't do to hide from her.

He glared at Killian as he moved around the desk. Since he wasn't about to drag one of the chairs there and waste everyone's time, he pushed Killian and sat on the arm of his chair. "Queen Ita. It's a pleasure to see you again. Thank you."

The human next to her beamed. "So the egg hatched?"

Tito nodded at Gideon. "Some time ago. My son is perfectly healthy."

"That's good."

For a few minutes, they talked about nothing of importance. Tito tapped his pen on his tablet, eager to get to the point of the meeting. He didn't want to rush Killian or the queen, but he needed to know what was going to happen.

"Tito is eager to know about the Saganto clan's wealth," Killian said.

Tito made a strangled noise and scowled at his friend. "Really?"

"What? You are. You've been asking about it almost every time we see each other, and you can finally find out what's happening."

"You make me sound like a gold digger."

Queen Ita chuckled. "I don't think that's what you sound like. It's understandable that you want to know what's happening, especially with the renovations. I really wish you'd let me pay for those, Killian."

Killian shook his head. "It was my father's fault that you had to rescue your clan members. The Eiloren clan will pay for the renovations connected to that."

Tito wished Killian would give in, too. It would free up a lot of money they could use in other ways.

Gideon cleared his throat. "Unfortunately, it'll take some time to assess just how wealthy the Saganto clan was. They spent a lot on the war effort, but that didn't make them a poor clan. The fact that they absorbed a lot of smaller clans added to their wealth. It's one of the reasons this is so complicated."

Tito must have made a face because Queen Ita leaned forward. "Why do you need that money so badly? Killian, I hope you know that if you need anything, you can ask me. I didn't have the best relationship with your father, but you're not him. Our clans are allies, and I want the Eiloren clan to thrive as much as the Ogorth clan is."

Tito didn't expect Killian to be honest. He should have known better, but he hadn't been there to see Killian and Queen Ita grow close. He'd been here, taking care of his egg. He didn't resent anyone for that, but sometimes, he wished he had all the information. It would be easier to predict what would happen.

"Since you knew my father, I'm sure you're aware of the kind of person he was," Killian explained. "He used the clan's wealth for his own benefit, and between the refugees and the renovations, and of course, the war, our coffers are empty. We have enough money to survive, but one of my brothers is making noise about taking my place on the throne, and having money problems isn't helping."

The queen didn't look happy. "We can't afford for someone else to take over the Eiloren clan."

"I'm not planning on allowing any of my siblings to take over."

"I could lend you money."

Killian shook his head. "I can't ask that of you. The Ogorth clan has its own rebuilding to do, and you took in a lot of refugees. I won't take money from you when you need it the most."

"What about that man who emailed us?" Gideon asked.

He was turned toward the queen, clearly talking to her, but Tito leaned forward. What man?

The queen frowned. "I thought we'd agreed it wouldn't be a good idea to allow him to move in with our clan."

"We did, but he didn't ask to move in with the Ogorth clan specifically."

"Can you explain what's going on?" Killian asked.

Tito was glad because he'd been about to ask the same thing, and it wasn't his place. He was just a personal assistant and shouldn't be talking to Queen Ita.

Gideon turned toward them. "I get emails like that almost every day. People want to move in with the clans. Most of the time, they're just curious about dragons, but sometimes, some of the emails are serious. I can tell that these people truly want a new start at life and to help the clans and humans integrate."

"And this email was one of those?"

"Yes. This guy is one of the richest men in the country. I almost dismissed the email because of that, but he's ready to contribute as much money as needed, as he made sure to write in his email. We were wary because the queen wondered if this was just another way for this guy to expand his business, but I don't think that's the case. Something in his email told me that he needs a big change and that he's ready to leave the human world behind."

Killian and Tito looked at each other. Tito wasn't sure he liked what he'd just heard, but this might be the only way for them to get out of this mess. At the very least, it would be worth talking to this man.

Killian turned back to the computer. "Tell me more."

Even though both Birch and Marlin were nearby, Oam couldn't help looking around as he walked into the dining hall.

He and Tito had talked. Tito had agreed that Oam and the babies shouldn't be locked away just because of what Filicia might be planning, and while he'd warned Oam to be careful and had assigned another bodyguard to him, he hadn't tried to change Oam's mind about leaving their rooms.

That was still weird to think. It hadn't taken much for Oam to move into Tito's rooms, and while they didn't quite feel like home yet, they would soon. The four of them already felt like family, after all.

"Oam!"

Oam looked up to see his sister waving at him. Dove was sitting with a group of friends, which would give Oam and the babies more protection. He'd agreed to have lunch with her and their friends because he missed them and because he hoped that Filicia wouldn't dare try anything if people surrounded him.

He moved toward her. Daron was in the carrier against Oam's chest while he was holding Sandor. Sandor was the quieter of the two, so Oam didn't expect him to try to wiggle out of his hold. The baby was content to look around from Oam's arms. On the other hand, Daron wouldn't have hesitated to launch herself onto the table, which was why she was trapped in the carrier.

Dove beamed when Oam reached her. "It's so good to see the three of you," she said as she tickled under Sandor's chin.

The baby chirped and looked at Oam. Oam wasn't sure what he was asking, but he nodded. To his surprise, Sandor reached for Dove, asking to be taken.

She looked delighted and quickly obeyed the silent order. She sat back down, cradling the baby against her chest, and Oam took the opportunity to do the same. He looked around the table, relaxing at every face he recognized.

"It feels like we haven't seen you in ages," Ash teased from his seat in front of Oam.

"That's because we haven't," Tibor said. "He's been locked away with his babies."

Ash knocked their shoulders together. "Yeah, but look how happy he is."

"That's probably thanks to a certain personal assistant to the king."

Oam's face flushed, and he knew he was blushing. He glared at his friends, but there was no heat behind it. He didn't mind that they teased him. He wasn't hiding his relationship with Tito, especially now that they'd moved in together.

Saya leaned over her plate. "Tell us about him."

A hand on his shoulder made Oam jerk away, but he relaxed when he saw it was Marlin. "Yes?"

"I'm going to get you some food. Do you have any preference?"

"I'll do that," Saya said as she got to her feet. "I know what he likes and doesn't like."

She winked at Marlin, who blinked at her and watched as she walked away. He stepped back, giving Oam space to be with his friends. Oam considered Marlin and Birch his friends, too, but he understood that right now, they were working and couldn't be distracted.

It would have been better for Oam not to be distracted, too, but he couldn't help it. He hadn't seen his friends in a long time and was happy to spend time with them. He was so focused on their stories that he didn't notice what was about to happen until he felt his sister tense next to him.

He looked up and froze when he saw Rutger's sister coming toward him. He wasn't sure what to make of her. She wasn't the one who kept threatening to take his daughter away, but she was still part of that family and Filicia's daughter. There could be nothing good in the reason she was coming toward him. There were other dragons with her, and Oam had no idea who they were. Probably more members of Rutger's family.

He sucked in a breath and got ready for whatever they were about to throw at him. He wished they would have avoided doing so in the dining hall in front of half the clan, but he supposed everyone knew what was going on already.

Before the group reached his table, two dragons sitting a few tables down got to their feet and blocked their way. Oam stared, wondering what they were doing. Juvia clearly felt the same because she tried walking past them, but they sidestepped her and blocked her way again.

"What are you doing?" she asked, sounding outraged that anyone would dare stop her.

"Leave Oam and his babies alone."

Oam blinked. Why were these dragons standing up for him? He'd seen them around the palace, but he'd never talked to them.

"Yeah, leave them alone," someone further in the room said. "He's those babies' father, and no one should take them from him. Stop hounding him."

"That child is my brother's daughter," Juvia said in a rising voice. "My family has a right to raise her."

"Your family has a right to fuck off," a third dragon said, causing several people in the room to snicker. "You're all horrible, and you shouldn't be allowed to raise any children."

More dragons started getting to their feet. Oam had no idea what to make of this, but he looked around in awe as Juvia and the dragons with her had to surrender. He couldn't see her anymore because of the many dragons standing between them.

"What's happening?" he asked in a whisper.

His sister leaned closer. "They're standing up for you."

"Why?" Oam knew most of these people by sight, but he wouldn't call them his friends.

"We all know Rutger's family and what they've been doing to you. It's not fair, and while I didn't expect all these people to stand up for you, I'm glad they did. If we don't do anything, Rutger's family will be allowed to do whatever they want, and no one wants that to happen."

Oam couldn't see Rutger's sister anymore, but he could still hear her. She was screaming to be allowed to pass, but a wall of dragons was now between them. Eventually, he heard her walk away. She was loudly telling anyone who would listen that they'd pay for what they'd done, and for a moment, Oam was worried. But as he looked around, he realized that whatever Filicia did to get revenge for what had happened, it would be impossible for her to hurt all these people. There were too many.

Oam didn't know how to thank them, but he realized he wouldn't have to. As they started sitting down again, one of the dragons who'd initially stood up for him turned to him and nodded. Oam nodded back, and the dragon went back to their meal without trying to talk to him.

Oam hadn't expected the clan to stand up for him, but they had. He'd always believed he'd be fighting Filicia and her family on his own, but now, he knew he wouldn't, and for the first time, he truly allowed himself to believe that he and his daughter would have a happy future. Being with Tito had helped, but what had just happened sealed the deal.

Tito didn't know what to think of what Gideon and Queen Ita were telling him and Killian. It sounded good, but maybe that was part of the problem. "I don't fully understand why he wants to move in with the clan. Why would he want to leave all of his life behind?" he asked.

Gideon shrugged. "Your guess is as good as mine. In his email, he explained that he lost someone important to him and is disgusted with how human authorities are dealing with what's been happening with the dragons."

Tito was, too. The humans had agreed to an alliance with the Ogorth clan and the clans who stood with them, but they hadn't been doing a lot to get rid of the hunters. The dragons had been focused on the war with the Saganto clan, so they hadn't done much about it, either, but maybe it was time to hold the humans to their word.

Luckily, that wasn't something Tito needed to worry about. It wasn't his place.

"It's strange to think that he cares about our well-being so much," he said.

"I've told you everything I know about him. I looked into him and found nothing that would tell me not to take him in. Queen Ita had the last say and decided it would be better to say no. We have enough to deal with without adding a rich human to it. It would be your best bet if you need money so desperately, though."

Tito was uncomfortable with the Ogorth clan knowing that, but he wasn't the one making decisions. Killian had told them. He wouldn't have done so if he didn't trust them. Tito just hoped Killian wouldn't make this decision without thinking about it.

"We're not that desperate yet," Killian said. "But I don't have anything against this man moving in with the clan as long as I can talk to him first. If we want dragons to integrate with humans, we have to show the world that we can live together. The Ogorth clan is doing a lot for that with all your humans, but you shouldn't be the only clan to have them."

Queen Ita grinned. "I always knew you were jealous of my humans."

Killian laughed. "Not jealous. More curious, and I can't wait to talk to this man."

Tito glanced down at his notes. The man's name was Hedley White, and Tito already had plans to look him up.

"As long as the right conditions are met and Mr. White is willing to follow our rules, I don't see a problem with him moving in with us after we talk," Killian continued.

Tito hoped they were doing the right thing but wouldn't know until they did it.

While Killian continued talking with Queen Ita and Gideon, Tito quickly googled Mr. White. He'd never heard that name before, but then he'd been focused on helping Killian take over the clan and the war with the Saganto clan for so long that he hadn't thought about much beyond what happened between the palace's walls.

He wasn't surprised to find that Mr. White was disgustingly rich. If he was a good person—something Tito wasn't sure of because who could have so much money and be a good person—it would be a massive change for their clan. If he agreed to help, it could mean the difference between Killian sitting on the throne and one of his siblings taking it from him. That was the only reason Tito was willing to give this a chance, and as he quickly compiled a file, he wondered if this was too good to be true. Mr. White was rich, but from what Tito could see, he'd inherited most of that wealth. There was gossip, but he couldn't find any proof of anything the man had done wrong. There were many articles about Mr. White losing his parents in a plane crash, which would explain what Gideon had said about him losing someone important.

Tito didn't know what Mr. White was looking for by moving in with a dragon clan, but he'd make sure to ask him when they met.

He was still worried even when the meeting was over. It was good to know they had allies, but there was much to think about and not a lot of time to do so. They needed to solve their problem with money before Filicia and Killian's brother found out about it and decided to use it against Killian.

Killian sent Tito home after the meeting, even though Tito still had work to do. For once, Tito didn't argue. He *wanted* to go home and see his family, so he quickly packed up his things and rushed down the hallways. He nodded at Marlin and Birch when he found them outside of his door, relieved to see they were protecting Oam. It was lucky that Killian felt he didn't need bodyguards around the palace, but both he and Tito knew that wasn't the case. Birch and Marlin needed to be reassigned to him, which meant Tito had to talk to the other guards and find someone he could trust with his family.

But not tonight. Tonight, he opened his front door and walked in. He smiled when he saw Oam playing with the babies on one of the carpets. The children ran for him as soon as they saw him, and Tito crouched so he could catch them when they reached him. He hauled them into his arms and twirled them around, laughing at their squeaks.

When he put them down, Oam was looking at them with a soft expression on his face. Tito leaned closer and kissed him. For a moment, everything was right in his world.

"You won't believe what happened in the dining hall today," Oam said as the babies scampered back to their toys. Sandor almost fell on his face, but Oam was quick to help him maintain his balance. He was a great father and didn't distinguish between Sandor and Daron.

"You met your friends?" Tito asked.

"Yes, and it was good to see them again. That's not what I'm talking about, though. Rutger's sister tried to talk to me."

Tito groaned. "I have to worry about his sister now, too? Was Filicia there?"

"No," Oam said as he guided Tito toward the couches. "But there were other dragons with her, probably more members of Rutger's family. You don't have to worry, though. Things were fine."

"Did Marlin and Birch have to step in?"

"No, because Juvia never reached me. A bunch of dragons blocked her and told her to leave me alone. They said I was the children's father and that I should be the one to raise them and basically told her to fuck off." Oam glanced at the children, but they were busy playing with a ball and hadn't heard him. "The clan supports me, Tito. They knew who Rutger was and what his family is like, and they made sure they couldn't hurt me. I thought I was alone, but I'm not."

Tito pulled Oam into his arms. "You never were and never will be."

He realized it was different for Oam to have the support of the rest of the clan. Tito was in love with Oam, so of course he supported him. The rest of the clan didn't feel anything like that, but they were still on his side. It was a victory for him.

But it didn't mean they could ignore Filicia. It was good to know that the clan would stand up for what was right, but she was dangerous, and Tito had enough of dealing with her and her temper tantrums. Something needed to be done so they could focus on whichever of Killian's brothers was stupid enough to think he could take the clan from Killian.

There would be a lot of work, but that was all right. Tito would do it with a smile because he'd do it to keep his family safe.

CHAPTER THIRTEEN

When there was a knock on the door, Tito considered not opening. He and Oam were going through Oam's things to decide what could stay in storage and what Oam wanted to display in their rooms. Tito had to store some of his things away, but he didn't mind. He wanted Oam to have his own space in the rooms they now shared, and it pleased him to see their things sitting next to each other.

It was the first time off he'd taken since the babies had been born. It was only one day, and he wanted to make the most of it. He and Oam had taken advantage of it his morning. They'd gotten up late and had spent the morning with the babies. Now, it was time to do a bit of work, but it was work Tito enjoyed. Oam would feel more settled and like he belonged in these rooms, which was what Tito wanted.

But someone was knocking on their door, which meant they were about to be interrupted. It could be one of their family members, but it could also be trouble, which was why Tito didn't want to open.

But he didn't have a choice. If he didn't see who it was, they would probably call, and he'd have to answer anyway.

He rose from the couch and kissed the top of Oam's head. "I'll see who it is. Stay here."

Oam nodded. He didn't even look up at Tito, focused as he was. That was fine with Tito. If it was trouble, he wanted Oam to stay away from it.

He opened the door, ready to defend his family, and blinked at the sight of Killian standing in the hallway. Tito looked behind him, not surprised to see Birch and Marlin there. The two guards assigned to Oam stood by the door, one on each side.

At least Killian wasn't going around on his own.

"Did we have a meeting I forgot about?" he asked.

Killian shook his head. "We didn't talk about this, but I thought it would be a good idea for you and Oam to have a housewarming party."

Tito could think of nothing worse. "It's only Oam moving in. I've lived in these rooms for a while." Ever since he and Killian had taken over the clan.

Killian rolled his eyes. "And you don't think that Oam moving in is worth celebrating?"

"Of course it is, but we don't need a party to do that."

"Well, you're going to have one anyway. I contacted Oam's friends and family, and they'll be arriving soon. I also had Samsa organize food and drinks. If you let us in, we'll set everything up. You won't have to raise one finger."

Tito narrowed his eyes. "What about cleanup?"

"Samsa has everything in hand. You don't have to worry about anything but be here and smile."

Tito grumbled as he stepped aside to let Killian in. Killian made it sound so easy, but Tito didn't feel like smiling. He felt like strangling his best friend.

Oam jumped to his feet as soon as he saw Killian. He hesitated, then bowed lightly before straightening again.

Killian laughed and strode toward Oam, pulling him into his arms and hugging him tight. "There's no need for you to bow. In fact, I don't want you to."

"I have no idea how to behave," Oam confessed. His cheeks were flushed.

Killian gave him an indulgent smile. "Forget I'm your king. As far as I'm concerned, you're my best friend's mate, which is all that matters. Treat me as if I was a friend, all right?"

Oam nodded. Knowing him, he'd slip now and then, but it was important to Killian that Oam treat him like he was just another dragon, and Tito was sure Oam understood that. He'd do what he could to make Killian happy.

Killian looked around. "The babies?"

"They're napping," Tito explained. "They should be up soon, but I don't know how they'll react to having so many people around."

"Daron will probably be fine, but we'll have to keep an eye on Sandor," Oam said. "I think they'll both be okay as long as it's only people close to us and not too many of them."

Killian raised his hands. "I promise I didn't invite half the clan. I called your sister, Oam, and she gave me a list of the people she thought needed to be here. Tito only has me because no one else likes him, so besides his parents, who said they'd be here, there wasn't anyone else to ask."

Tito glared. "I don't need more friends with you in my life. You're giving me too many headaches as it is."

For a while, Tito had thought he'd never have this again. He'd been convinced Killian would be killed during the fight with the Saganto clan, and he didn't know how he would have dealt with that. The thought of losing his best friend terrified him, and he told himself he didn't have to be worried anymore. The war was over. Killian was safe and sound.

Tito and Oam didn't have time to prepare. Someone knocked on the door, and after that, it was a steady stream of people until everyone was there. Tito kept a close eye on Oam and the babies once they woke up, but he could see they were more relaxed than he was, even Sandor, who looked at home in the arms of Oam's sister.

Their family was surrounded by people who loved them and would support them through anything Filicia and the rest of Rutger's family would put them through. It was good to see, but it was even better to hear Oam's laughter and to see how happy he was.

Tito knew that Oam had felt alone before. After what had happened with Rutger, he'd put distance between himself and his friends. It had probably hurt a lot to have to go through a pregnancy only to give up the egg, and instead of relying on his friends to help him through it, he'd isolated himself. Tito couldn't blame him. He did the same when he had a problem, no matter how many times Killian told him to stop being an asshole. Tito dealt fine with things alone, but that wasn't the case for Oam.

It was a good thing he'd never be alone again.

"Do you know why I organized a surprise party?" Killian asked as he swung an arm around Tito's shoulders.

Tito grumbled but leaned against his friend's side. "Because if you'd told me about it, I would have said no."

Killian chuckled. "Exactly. I know you don't like parties and being the center of attention more than you already are, but this wasn't just for you. It was for you and Oam, and I thought it would be good for him to see how many people love and support him."

"Sometimes, I wonder how you can be king, but then, you say something smart, and I remember that you're not as stupid as you act."

Killian squeezed Tito before releasing him. "Damn right. I'm smart. And to show you just how smart I am, I'll tell you that I think that sometimes, you need to be reminded of the people who care about you, too."

Maybe Killian was right. Tito didn't have many people he trusted, but they all were here today. Killian was there, along with Marlin, Birch, and Tito's family.

And now, there was also Oam, the babies, Oam's family, and his friends. Tito's world had expanded in a way he hadn't expected after he'd allowed Oam into his life, and he wouldn't have it any other way.

What did one do when their king threw them a party? Oam wouldn't have known how to answer that question before, but now, he did. When your king threw you a party, you smiled and went along with it.

He didn't mind. He didn't understand why Killian felt it was important, but he loved being surrounded by the people who mattered the most to him. He'd pushed them away after he'd gotten pregnant, mostly because he hadn't known how to deal with what was happening to him. They wouldn't have judged him, but they would have pitied him and tried to help even though there had been nothing any of them could have done. Oam had needed time to process what was happening, but all that was over now. He had his children, Tito, and all the people around him. He had new friends, including Killian.

That was going to take some time getting used to.

Ash bumped their shoulders together, startling Oam out of his thoughts. He quickly looked around for the children, relieved to see Sandor in his sister's arms while Daron played on the floor with Twig and Tibor.

"Would you ever have thought the *king* would throw you a party?" Ash asked.

Oam shook his head. "Or that he'd be my friend."

"Yeah, it's weird. Imagine if his father were still king."

Oam couldn't. Things would have been so different if Killian hadn't rebelled against his father and taken the throne. Oam would have been kept away from his daughter. He wouldn't have found Tito, and they wouldn't be in love. He wouldn't have Sandor.

He didn't want to imagine what his life would be like.

"Happiness looks good on you," Ash said. He was smiling softly.

Oam knew he'd made his friends worry. He'd worried himself sometimes, too. All of that was in the past, and he wanted his family to know that.

"I'm fine," he reassured Ash.

"You are, and it's good to see. Don't do that again, though. If you need us, talk to us. We're all here for you. We love you."

Oam hugged him. "I'm sorry."

"It's fine. It was just scary for a moment, but it's over."

That wasn't quite the truth. Filicia and the rest of Rutger's family were still out there, probably plotting how to get their paws on Daron. Oam was terrified because Filicia wouldn't hesitate to attack Killian head-on and support whichever of Killian's siblings wanted the throne. It was as if she couldn't see how bad things would be if Killian were to lose the throne. Maybe she did see it but didn't care. She wanted Daron, and that was all that mattered to her.

Oam felt he'd created trouble for Killian and the clan, no matter how many times Tito reassured him that whatever Filicia did wasn't his responsibility. He was right, and logically, Oam knew that. It didn't help him feel any less guilty when he thought of what the consequences could be, though.

But he needed to have faith. No matter what Filicia came up with, he wouldn't be alone facing her. Killian, Tito, and their friends and families would support Oam, just like they would support Killian if someone attacked him and the throne. There wasn't much Oam would be able to do, but he'd still be there like Killian was there for him now.

Ash drifted away, and eventually Oam found himself with both babies. Sandor was draped around Oam's neck, his eyes drooping, while Daron had stretched out in Oam's arms. She was tired but still looked around with interest as if trying to take in everything happening around her. Oam could already tell she'd be trouble when she grew up, but she was still young. He loved that her favorite place was his arms and that he could cuddle her like this.

He stroked her back, content to sit on the couch as he watched everyone around him have fun. He wasn't surprised when Tito found him and sat next to him. He leaned sideways, and Tito wrapped an arm around his shoulders and pulled him close to kiss his temple.

"I see the troublemakers are sleepy," Tito said.

"It's a lot for them. I like that they took this so well, though."

Tito nodded. "These people are their family."

They were, and if anything were to happen to Oam and Tito, the babies would still be protected. Oam knew that Tito had done everything in his power to make sure of that. He'd had Oam sign all the necessary documents so Oam could rest easier. Dove and Killian would take the babies and raise them as Tito and Oam would have.

But nothing was happening to anyone, at least not today. Oam relaxed against Tito's side and turned to kiss his cheek. Tito grinned and turned his head so that their lips met.

Oam rolled his eyes. "You could just have asked for a kiss."

"What would be the fun in that?"

This *was* fun. For a long time, Oam hadn't felt that way, but he did now, and he wouldn't lose this. The babies and Tito, along with their families, were his future.

A rosy future Oam hadn't thought he'd have.

EPILOGUE

"He's here," Samsa said as she opened the door of Killian's office.

Tito stopped pacing and straightened his back. What was about to happen could make or break the clan.

He hated that a human had the power to do that, but they didn't have a choice. Killian had to listen to what Hedley White had to say, and once he had, he'd have to decide if he'd allow the man to become a clan member.

Killian was sitting behind his desk. He was nervous, but Tito could see it only because he knew him so well. Mr. White wouldn't see it, which hopefully would play in their favor.

"Give us a few minutes, then let him in," Killian told Samsa.

She nodded and closed the door again, and Killian turned to Tito. "Will you sit down? You're making me anxious."

"You're being ridiculous, but fine." Tito always felt better pacing and burning his nervous energy, but he wasn't the one who mattered here. That was Killian, and Tito would do what he could so that Killian was settled. If that meant sitting down, that was what he'd do.

He turned one of the chairs by Killian's desk so he'd see Mr. White better. Killian was on his side of the desk, tapping his fingertips on the wooden surface. The sound made Tito want to snap at him to stop, but luckily, he didn't have to listen to it for long. A few moments later, Samsa knocked on the door again, and Killian went from a nervous mess to a king who was sure of himself and of what he was doing.

"Come in," he called out.

The door opened, and a man walked in. Tito had re-searched Mr. White, so he knew what he looked like, but he was more handsome face to face.

Tito remembered reading that Mr. White was six foot two, and while that was short next to most dragons, it gave the man an imposing presence. He wore a suit that was obviously custom-made, and his hair was neatly cut and combed. It was graying on the sides, but that was normal since Mr. White was in his mid-forties.

The man glanced around the room before his gaze stopped on Killian. Tito could see intelligence in his eyes and hoped this man would be on their side. They'd be in trouble if he decided to support Killian's enemies.

Mr. White stopped in front of the desk and bowed. "Your Majesty. Thank you for allowing me to visit your clan and for agreeing to this meeting."

"Please, call me Killian."

Tito glared at Killian. Would it be too much to ask him to do things correctly?

Mr. White blinked, appearing surprised. "Are you sure?"

"I am. I haven't been a king for long, and I'd rather have people call me by my name. This is Tito, my assistant. I hope you don't mind, but I asked him to sit in on this meeting."

Mr. White turned to Tito and nodded. Tito nodded back. "You can call me Tito."

Mr. White chuckled. "Then I insist you call me Hedley."

"That won't be a problem," Killian said as he gestured for Hedley to sit.

He did so in the only chair left, crossing one leg over the other and settling in as if he belonged there.

Tito hadn't known what to expect, but to his surprise, he felt at ease. Hedley didn't feel like a threat. That didn't mean he wasn't, and Tito would be careful, but he hoped it was a good sign. He'd expected a rich and arrogant man full of himself who would make demands, but that didn't seem to be the case.

"Gideon told me a bit about your request," Killian said. "He explained that you want to move in with a dragon clan and are ready to support whatever clan will welcome you with your considerable wealth."

Hedley linked his fingers and dropped his hands on his knee. "That's correct. I realize I'm extremely lucky, and not because of anything I did. I was born into this wealth but never needed all this money. I've been giving to charities since I inherited my father's company and assets, but sometimes it feels like I can't give away money quickly enough. The company is successful."

Tito wanted to glare at the human but kept his expression smooth. Oh, what a problem Hedley had that he couldn't give away his money fast enough before more of it appeared in his bank account.

"Do you see our clan as charity, then?" Killian asked.

Hedley shook his head. "That's not what I meant. I've spent most of my life focused on work and making more money. It's how I was raised, and I didn't see anything odd in that way of thinking. I would have continued behaving that way until I had a heart attack or a breakdown, but when the news of dragons came out, I realized there was so much more in the world than what I knew. No matter how much I travel and how much money I have, my world is tiny. It's focused on the company and nothing else, but I want to see more."

"There's a big step from realizing that to deciding you want to leave the human world behind," Tito pointed out.

Hedley was still relaxed as he answered. "It is. All my life, I had everything I wanted except for one thing. I never felt like I belonged anywhere. I didn't belong with my family or at college. I only have a few friends. Focusing on work was much easier than building meaningful relationships with them. I don't want to do that anymore. I want to change and for people to benefit from my wealth. If I become a member of your clan, I'll share all of it with you. That's how it works, isn't it? Every clan member contributes to the clan's wealth, and in turn, the clan helps those who need it and protects everyone."

Killian nodded. "That's how it's supposed to work. I'm going to be honest with you. As I told you before, I haven't been the king for long. My father sat on the throne before me, and he wasn't a good ruler. Between the years he was on the throne and the war, our clan is in trouble, and having your wealth at our disposal would solve all our problems. I don't want to take advantage of you, though, and I'm not sure what you'll get from becoming a clan member."

"Let me put it like this. How would you feel if you didn't have a clan?"

"I wouldn't know what to do with myself. I was born in this clan. I belong here."

Tito felt the same. He knew humans didn't have clans, but he couldn't imagine what life was like for them. They had to feel alone.

Sometimes, he wished he could be alone, but then, he remembered that he wouldn't have so many people who loved him if he was. Being part of the clan meant he had to deal with people he wished he never had to talk to, like Filicia, but it was worth it if it also gave him Oam and their family.

"*I* never belonged anywhere," Hedley explained. "I'm an only child, and neither of my parents were ever interested in raising me. They left me with nannies until I was old enough to be sent off to boarding school. I made a few friends here and there, but I was always a loner, and not because I wanted to be one. I'm not saying I'll fit in perfectly with your clan, and I realized that as a human, I might bring you more trouble than I'm worth, but I just want a chance. I want to feel a part of something important, to build a family, and to find a place where I belong. I was never able to find that with humans."

"And you believe you might find it with dragons," Killian finished.

Hedley nodded once. "I hope so. At the very least, it's worth trying."

Tito and Killian looked at each other. Killian would make the final decision, but like always in important situations, he wanted to know what Tito thought of it.

Hedley White could be the solution to most of the clan's problems, but he might also bring more trouble than they could deal with. Unfortunately, there was only one way to find out which way things would go.

ABOUT THE AUTHOR

Catherine is the creator of several series, most of them paranormal, including the Whitedell Pride Series and the Gillham Pack Series. While she graduated in translation, she decided to go the writer's way because it was more fun to create her own stories and characters.

She's been living in Italy for more than twenty years, but she's a daughter of the North—Belgium to be precise—and she misses it so much that she's already planning to move back.

She loves pizza—probably too much—her son, her pets, and of course, books. She sneaks some reading time into her schedule every time she has five minutes free from writing, demands from her various pets and son, and lastly, housework.

Connect with her:

lievens.catherine@gmail.com
BookBub: https://www.bookbub.com/authors/catherine-lievens
Website: https://authorcatherinelievens.com/
Facebook: https://www.facebook.com/catherine.lievens.9
Facebook Group: https://www.facebook.com/groups/411788002341528/
Twitter: https://twitter.com/authorCLievens
Newsletter: http://eepurl.com/c-uvKn